Praise fo~ ~p~

"Melisa is a gifted and highly accomplished therapist who partners with her equally gifted, pure, powerful horses. Melisa bridges heart and soul from horses to humans to create energetic magic allowing clients to face life's most tender issues with sure-footed ease by creating a powerful environment to heal in unconditional love. She has translated the essence of her day job into a captivating fairy tale. *Eponalisa* is for our inner child and for children as well. We are taken on a journey of self-discovery where there is joy in investigating our gifts and honoring our strengths. Deeply connected with the spirits of the horses who live with her, Melisa creates a wonderfully authentic horse story turned fantasy with understandable, approachable archetypes lightly woven with the lovely use of color, light, images of fairies, jewels and the chakras. It is a magical, meaningful look at recognizing, connecting with and supporting the most important qualities in each of us."
Molly K. Campbell, Prosperity Guide, Healer, and former Wall Street Banker

"*Eponalisa* is a whimsical fairy tale that has the ability to touch the reader with very real and important lessons which can be applied to everyday life. The journey with a magical horse, Wisdom, and his appointed fairy, Eponalisa, takes the reader through lessons that are filled with adventure and enjoyment. The prose is written in a way that draws the reader into the journey—setting

off smells, sights and sounds—thus proving to be a very ethereal adventure of the senses. Both a quaint bedtime story and a silent escape from your day, *Eponalisa* is a delightful voyage for horse lovers of all ages."
Valerie L. Young, Publisher, *Horse Connection Magazine*

"*Eponalisa* offers a timeless, take-me-away moment with characters that seem all at once magical and real. It's a perfect coming-of-age and awareness book for young girls (and boys)."
AJ Grant, President, Big Green Company/ Big Green Rabbit

"It's a beautiful thing to follow your passion. I feel so blessed to get to do what I love. Whether you are searching for your personal calling or are already fortunate enough to know your path, Melisa Pearce's book will inspire you to dig even deeper to find your joy. You truly will be 'touched' by a girl and a horse. Jane, Beau (my Wisdom and Clarity), and I give this magical work a heartfelt hooves and thumbs up!"
Templeton Thompson, Award Winning Recording Artist

"What an incredible journey Eponalisa takes us on! Leave it to Melisa Pearce to provide an opportunity to rediscover that twelve-year-old kid inside ourselves and allow her to magically transform into an empowered and compassionate being. How fun it is to read a modern day fairy tale that reminds us grown-ups of our own talents, purpose and the important reasons for being here. Ride on, Eponalisa!"

Leah Juarez, Publisher/Editor, *Equesse Magazine* for women who love horses

"As an educational consultant, I know the importance of stories that guide and teach. As the father of an eleven-year-old girl who loves horses, I know how hard it is to find such stories. With *Eponalisa*, Melisa Pearce has given us a simple tale that combines magic, myth, and wisdom into a fun and enjoyable story. I cannot wait to give this book as a gift to my daughter!"

Rob Meltzer, MA, CEP, Educational Consultant, Founder of Northlight Family Services

"Insightful, calming, and thoroughly enjoyable. What better path to understand ourselves and our four legged friends than through the astute eyes of Melisa Pearce, a true revelator. The descriptions and analogies reflect the remarkable perception Melisa has of the horse world and how it resonates with us as individuals. Congrats on a great piece!"

Jan Guynn, Youth Advisor for the Rocky Mountain Reining Horse Association and Youth Committee Member for the Rocky Mountain Quarter Horse Association

"Melisa Pearce captures the essence of relationship in this moving fairy tale. She covers it all—relationships with nature, animals, family, and most importantly, with our Self and our higher calling—as she very adroitly weaves life lessons into a fanciful ride. Along the way, she places little nuggets of sound horsemanship that will help any person working with horses build a more solid and effective partnership. She also helps to outline the role that horses play in humanity's evolution. As someone who has experienced her work with horses and humans, I can attest to the fact that what she teaches is what she lives. Well done!"

Amy Skolen, leadership coach, CEO of Unbridled Performance: The Center for Team and Leadership Breakthroughs

"I found the story enchanting. Through the persona of Eponalisa, we can see our different roles and purposes in life. The journey allowed me to recognize the many aspects of our lives—as mother, daughter, teacher, and caregiver—and how important it is to also play in our lives. It is a story that will draw the reader in with magic and fun."

Ms. Lisa Adams, M Ed.

"Melisa has found a beautiful way to speak to a young girl through her passion for horses. Based on Melissa's lifelong experience with horses and a deep understanding of the qualities that make a fine human being, *Eponalisa* weaves a story of longing and belonging. Melisa's words transform a tale into the qualities we seek in our human journey, whether we are young or simply young at heart."

Nancy Lowrey, Founder of The Natural Leader Equine Program

"Melisa has captured, in a unique and soul melting fashion, a fantasy grounded by strong moral messages, delivered by a vehicle so easy to adopt in our young consciousness that we find ourselves loping along with the Fairy Eponalisa and Wisdom, sharing the task of giving these treasures to the deserving. A definite feel-good read with the power to demand that you look to and question your inner self, if not your total being."

Mark E. Guynn, Trainer, Clinician, NRHA,
NRCHA and AQHA Special Events Judge

"Even if you are not an animal lover (as we are), you will be inspired by Melisa's touching story of discovering one's personal calling in life through a journey with a magical horse. Animals can tell us so much about ourselves . . . if only we will listen."

Hilton and Lisa Johnson, founders of Health-
CoachTraining.com and GlobalTeleClass.com

"*Eponalisa* is a rich fantasy with the power to bring horse wisdom into reality for all who choose to go on the adventure."

June Gunter, Ed.D., Founder of TeachingHorse
and author of *TeachingHorse; Rediscovering Leadership*

"Melisa has captured a young girl's heart with this story and found a lovely way through her magical journey to teach some very valuable life lessons. Love, acceptance and compassion for others are three wonderful themes throughout her journey. When finished, readers will feel joyful and uplifted.

Larry Freeborg, Founder of Stepping Through the Gate

"The magic is in the journey. We enjoyed following Eponalisa and Wisdom as they sprinkled their fairy dust and showed how celebrating our uniqueness is the way to affirm our life purpose."

Roger Strachan, PhD, and Mado Reid,
Co-Directors, Center for Creative Choice

"This book should be required reading for both children and adults. Melisa transports us to a land of Life's Most Important Lessons. It is a valuable and sensitive perspective on our relationships with others, both human and animal."

John White, Certified John Lyons Horse Trainer

"The child in us yearns to live full out and make a profound difference. This is the transformation of Lisa to *Eponalisa*. And so it is with Melisa in her life and work. This is her Calling.

Peggy MacArthur, Therapist, friend and colleague
in life and work

Eponalisa

Melisa Pearce

Eponalisa

By
Melisa Pearce

Touched By A Horse™, Inc.

Eponalisa
By Melisa Pearce
Copyright © 2009 by Melisa Pearce

ISBN 13: 978-0-9760415-3-5
Library of Congress Control Number: 2008910552

Published by Touched By A Horse™, Inc.
Printed in the United States of America
First Edition
January, 2009
www.touchedbyahorse.com

Cover Illustration: Jan Taylor (http://www.jantaylor.com)
Cover and book design: Nick Zelinger, NZ Graphics
(http://www.nzgraphics.com)
Map and interior illustrations: Diane Halenda
Editing: Melanie Mulhall, Dragonheart
(http://www.thatcopywriter.com)
Proofreading: Helena Mariposa, Dragon Ink Productions

This book is dedicated to all horses. Living in my barn or yours, I thank these wise members of the Equine Realm for all the life lessons they have taught me. Whether they be draft or mini, competition or farm, Western or English, rodeo or show, racing or trail, domestic or wild . . . fantasy or real . . . I send my deepest gratitude to them.

ACKNOWLEDGMENTS

I stand in admiration of my talented friend, the equine artist, Jan Taylor (http://www.jantaylor.com) who placed my vision upon canvas, thanks to her immense gift as an artist. Thank you, Jan. Your incredible art has served me as a muse for my writing. The story of Eponalisa began to unfold on the day I saw how you had captured the pure essence of my dream. Thank you, too, for the beauty you share with the world through your gift.

Each step of the writing process was a thrill. I could hardly wait to share it with my closest friends and supporters. I wish to thank my personal assistant and great friend, Diane Halenda, for her shared interest and excitement about each twist and turn that poured forth, chapter by chapter. I am so grateful for all your hard work in keeping our other projects rolling while I worked to bring this book to fruition. Your constant belief in me, your friendship, and your encouragement about all my creative endeavors has truly been the wind beneath my own wings.

When Peggy MacArthur came into my life, I knew in my heart she was heaven-sent. Her strength and conviction as a coach and a friend have been truly amazing. From correcting typing errors and proofing the first draft to discussing the story line and suggesting ideas for me to ponder, Peggy's dedication to the project has been immense.

Peggy, you also encouraged me to find the precious time to get the project prioritized and not hidden under the many other projects I had going simultaneously. The fact that you are so committed to getting things exactly, precisely right every single time has made this book appreciably better. I am grateful for your early and ongoing review of the manuscript and your invaluable suggestions to improve it. Without your friendship and encouragement, Peggy, I may never have gotten my dream captured and turned into the paper reality of this book. I thank you.

I wish to thank my editor, Melanie Mulhall (http://www.thatcopywriter.com), for her heart of a dragon and loving spirit of a horse. Melanie, your professionalism and directness have given me the guidance needed to polish the story for the reader. I write as I speak and your spit and polish have brought out the shine. Thank you.

As you have under-promised and clearly over-delivered your gifts to the work, I thank you for your insight in guiding me through the tricky waters of editing and producing this book. I look forward to many more projects with you in the future and our new and deepening friendship.

Helena Mariposa, thank you for your detailed proofing, which is a talent in its own right. I should probably hire you full-time to follow me around.

And a thank you also goes out to Nick Zelinger (http://www.nzgraphics.com), who pulled together the look and feel of the cover and interior design of the book. Nick, I admire your patience with the selectiveness I felt in this stage of the process. I felt you honored that I was choosing for Spirit as well as for myself. You made the process easy and fun. Thank you.

I acknowledge my mother, who is, herself, a truly gifted artist. I am certain I received my creative gene from her. Mom, you always told me I could do anything or be anyone if I put my mind to it. I believed you, Mom. Thank you, Mom, for this and so much more.

I wish to thank my children—Cody, Molly and Kevin—for always supporting me and being proud of me as a mom. Even more than that, I am thankful to you for making it so easy for me to be proud of each of you. You are each a shining star in your own right and what I am most touched by in my life.

I am truly blessed to have a life partner and sweetheart, Dane, who understands me, cares for me, and is never resentful of the time I devote to my focused endeavors. Dane, I am grateful to you for so many things. Where this book is concerned, I am, most of all, grateful that you made sure I was balancing my work life with fun and laughter. You have a loving way of making sure I never take myself too seriously. I will always remember our days away together at the romantic B& B where I finished my writing by day and played on the town with you at night. You are my sweetheart, my confidant, and my best friend.

I am sure there are many others who I could thank from the bottom of my heart for your support, love and friendship in a myriad of ways in my life. A life with many animals, children, and businesses—as well as one that is no stranger to crisis—is only as sweet as mine when seasoned generously with good friends. I thank you all and hope you enjoy the ride!

Melisa

FOREWORD

Your vision will become clear only when
you can look into your own heart.
Carl Jung

In a dream one night, I saw the Fairy Eponalisa with such clarity that she stayed with me for several days. It was one of those dreams that makes me question a value or a principle I am living by in my life. I understood her message but not her assignment to write a book.

In my waking life, I had been approached by several clients and friends who knew that through my life's work with horses and my career as an equine facilitator, I had become an example of a person who was successfully living her passion. They consulted with me to discover how they could do the same. They asked, "How does one know their true life's calling? Will I recognize it? And even if I think I know what it is, how do I trust enough to follow it?" They were struggling with these questions and many more. I also met people who knew their calling and could feel their passion, but realized that their calling was not a career focused mission. They wondered if they were missing out somehow. I knew that my dream was somehow related to these waking reality inquiries.

I am blessed to have continually made choices in my life to be an entrepreneur and have consistently followed my passions. Those choices and passions have not always taken me on straight, clear trails. In fact, I have frequently chosen paths that have been circuitous, but which later gave me a piece of what I was eventually meant to do with my work. I did not see the beauty of each part of the path at every turn. Sometimes I chose work simply because I knew I could do it successfully and knew it would pay the bills. But even those projects and ventures have played a big part in all that I do today. As I formed that understanding, I often heard my mother's voice saying something I often heard in childhood: *Nothing one ever learns turns out to be wasted.* My mother was right.

The understandings and skills I picked up along the way all prepared me to do my life's work with my horses and my work with people as a healer, a guide, a coach, a teacher, a trainer, and a marketer. Those understandings and skills, put in place over a long period of time and through many experiences, were the pieces that have formed the whole puzzle picture of my own calling.

Over time, I have learned to simply say, "Yes." It is a "yes" to Spirit, an affirmation that I am here to serve, that I am available for Spirit's requests. I have watched for guidance and have trusted that when I leap, the net will, in fact, be there. And it always has been. That is how I have come to live my passion.

I described the fairy dream to my artist friend, Jan Taylor, and when she placed Eponalisa upon her canvas, I understood it was a story I was being asked to tell.

I honored that request. It is my intention to illuminate the path for you with this book, to place a few breadcrumbs on the path through the telling of this story.

This book is written for all those who are somewhere on the path, collecting pieces of their lessons and preparing for a future they may not even see today. Trust that it is a future that will hold passion and conviction and which will always, always, always be filled with white light. What you are becoming is always more important than what you are accomplishing.

TABLE OF CONTENTS

Our lives are shaped and seasoned by unforeseen circumstances. Our being human means we choose our own responses and reactions to them . . . often maturing as we grow. Through friendships and with guidance, our own truth is formed as we step into our destiny. Horses can be your dearest guides, most profound teachers and sweet, trusted confidants on life's journey.

Blessed are those of us who experience the whispers from a horse's heart.

~ Melisa Pearce

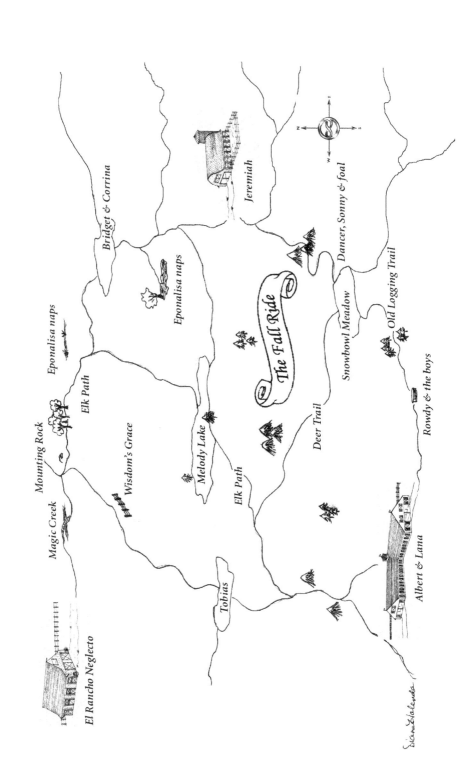

Part I:
The Transformation

CHAPTER ONE

The glare from the classroom windows didn't seem to bother Lisa's eyes as she stared out at the autumn leaves just beginning to abandon the trees. Her seventh grade homeroom class seemed so long some afternoons she could scream as she watched the clock hands slowly advance with a loud ticktock.

Friday afternoon had finally arrived. This was one of those special Friday afternoons when her parents were out of town and her grandma was standing in for them. The most exciting things always happened when her Grandma, whom she affectionately called Nana, stayed with her.

Seventh grade was a confusing time for Lisa. Her parents stressed the importance of school and getting a good education, but all she really wanted to do was be at the boarding barn doing absolutely anything with her horse, Clarity. School came easily for her, although she often wondered how any of the subjects they were studying would lead her to a career with horses. Both of her parents encouraged her to remember that horses were only a hobby. They spoke of and encouraged her to look at many types of careers, including those in small offices, big businesses, and hospitals. Lisa was not excited about pursuing any of these. All she wanted to do was find a way to make her life with a barn full of horses.

But now it was Friday and she could leave school and her worries about a career behind her. With her parents gone and Nana in charge, she knew it would be an adventurous weekend!

After briefly focusing on what her teacher was saying about her homework assignment, Lisa returned to her daydreaming as she gazed through the window. In only a few more days, all the leaves would be on the ground and the first snowfall would be upon them. Lisa wanted to get as much riding in on the weekend as possible. Lucky for her, Nana understood how important it was to her. She would conquer all her homework that evening and get to the barn early in the morning.

Nana would pack a wonderful lunch for her saddlebag and sweet snacks for Clarity, too. Nana had the best recipes for horse treats and cookies. Lisa knew, as she sat in class, that Nana was home baking treats for Clarity and a batch or two of chocolate chip cookies for her.

Planning it all out in her head, Lisa grew more and more anxious for the bell to ring. She would rise early in the morning, leave a sweet note for Nana, grab both her backpack of treats and her journal to document the trip, and walk the mile to the barn. Then she and Clarity would spend the day looking for adventure.

Lisa was halfway to the door by the time the bell had stopped ringing.

CHAPTER TWO

Awakening earlier than usual the next morning, Lisa stretched and wondered for a moment why she could feel so wide awake on a Saturday morning. On school mornings, she was so sleepy that she needed an alarm clock to awaken. She decided she would figure that one out later.

Picking up her leather journal, she quickly read what she had entered in it before falling to sleep the previous night.

Dear Me,

I can hardly believe how long we had to wait for the weekend! I could hardly pay attention at all. Mom left me a note for the weekend with the usual: behave (when don't I?), do your chores . . . blah, blah, blah. The usual lecture. Then she went on with what I already know: mind Nana and do your schoolwork.

I am so mad. She never even mentioned that I should have fun at the barn. It is as if she forgets about Clarity. I know she hates how dirty I get there, how my nails are not perfect, and the fact that I would rather have new boots than dresses.

I wish she would listen to me. I want to be with horses forever! Somehow, I want to be with horses as my job. I don't know what I will be but I cannot have any of the careers my parents push me towards. Maybe I will be a vet or a horse trainer.

I want them to be proud of me, but being with the horses is the only time I feel . . .

The journal seemed to stop abruptly. Lisa knew she had fallen asleep in mid-thought. Throwing back the covers and taking the journal with her, she climbed from her warm nest. Her feet hit the cool wood floor and her heart lifted as she remembered it was Saturday.

She combed her unruly hair into a long, thick brunette ponytail that hung to the middle of her back. Then she removed her retainer, placed it into its pink plastic case, and brushed her teeth. As an afterthought, she creamed her young skin. Lisa was not as interested in fashion or makeup as some of her friends, but she gave herself a small touch of mascara to bring out her hazel eyes and a wipe of lip gloss to moisten her lips. A mere half hour after jumping out of bed, she was ready to go out the door. Dressed in her favorite faded riding jeans, lavender t-shirt, white visor and boots, she was ready for anything.

She wrote a quick note of promise to Nana that she would give a check-in wave or leave a note at the Billings' farmhouse. Nana had asked her old friends at the nearby Billings farm to give her a call to say all was well when they saw Lisa ride by or found a note from her on their bulletin board. It was a small gesture for Lisa and she readily agreed to ride by their place, as she was grateful to have the freedom.

Nana had supplied some lemon yellow stationery and envelopes with little daisies printed on them for Lisa to write her notes to the family. Their daughter, who was a little younger than Lisa, had been home sick from school. Lisa wrote a tender note in her best penmanship, tucked it perfectly into an envelope, and placed it into her daypack. She added a few other essentials for her day with Clarity. Then she grabbed her daypack, tied her jacket around her small waist, and stepped outside to begin her walk to the barn.

Watching the sunrise over the fairway outside her parents' home, Lisa shook her head. Lisa believed that her parents had lacked the good sense to buy a farm. Instead, they lived on the side of one big waste of pretty grass—a golf course. Taking a shortcut across fairway seven on the nine-hole course, Lisa walked swiftly north toward the boarding barn.

The barn was located on a little alfalfa farm Lisa's mother had dubbed *El Rancho Neglecto* because it was in need of repair. But it always seemed perfect to Lisa and she dismissed her mother's opinion about it. Her parents had no interest in horses, but they paid the bills for Clarity's boarding and shoeing. They also were willing to give her lifts to the barn after school. As long as Lisa did well in school, was safe and had fun, they would support her passion even though they did not understand it. Lisa was glad they were not really involved. After all, it was her passion and she felt happily in charge of the situation.

Lisa walked swiftly. She couldn't wait to see Clarity. She cut through fields and finally came to the edge of the two-lane paved road she needed to cross at the farm's entrance. Lisa looked carefully in both directions. There were no cars in sight. Jogging across the blacktop and up the gravel driveway, she was sure Clarity sensed that she was coming.

She had arrived so early that even the farmhand, Paul, had not yet risen for the day. The farm was quiet; at least it was until Lisa opened the barn door. Upon hearing the squeak and roll of the big door, all the horses came to their stall gates in hungry anticipation that Paul had arrived early to feed them. Each horse seemed deeply disappointed as she walked by, so Lisa promised them all that Paul would be up soon with their breakfast. Clarity hung his head over the stall gate and watched her small frame walk up the concrete barn aisle. He nickered a welcome to his friend in happy recognition.

Paul had left Clarity's hay outside his stall in a small wheelbarrow, along with his can of molasses grain, just as Lisa had requested. Lisa tossed Clarity his hay, dumping his grain on top like a salad dressing. When she finished, she smiled, realizing she had started a nicker and whinny riot from all of Clarity's equine friends.

While her friend was munching his breakfast, she went to the tack room to prepare all the items they would need for the day. She picked up Clarity's halter and lead rope, along with her wooden caddy of grooming supplies, and went back to his stall.

Grooming Clarity was a vital first step. Lisa always wanted him to look and feel his best. It was a relief that the flies were gone for the year, as the nights had begun to get too cold for them to survive. Removing his blanket and hanging it over the stall door, Lisa began their usual routine. First, she took her dandy brush and went over his body thoroughly, in short, quick strokes. She was especially careful to groom him and check where she would place the saddle pad and cinch. His winter coat was beginning to grow in. As usual, its hue was from a different color palette than his summer coat.

Next, she gently took the braids out of his long mane. She knew Clarity loved to have his long mane free and flowing when they went on adventure rides. It was a mass of curls from the braids and looked full and beautiful to Lisa. When she took the braids out of his tail, Lisa shook it free to produce the same curly, full effect. Clarity was so beautiful to her. Every inch of him was her most precious treasure. He was her best friend and her most trusted confidant.

As she completed her grooming, she told Clarity about their day ahead. "Easy, boy. I'll wait for you to finish your breakfast and then we're going to go out for the whole day. We can explore and have adventures all day, as long as we're back to the barn before dark. All we need to do is stop off at the Billings farm. They're Nana's friends. As long as we do that, we are free to explore all we want! And Nana packed some great snacks."

Lisa patted his neck, then returned to the tack room for his saddle and tack. She slipped his bridle and reins over her shoulder and carried the saddle pad. Returning to the stall, she hung the saddle pad over the wheelbarrow by the stall gate and hooked the bridle on his stall latch.

On a second trip to the tack room, Lisa placed the cinch up over the saddle's seat and hooked the right stirrup up over the saddle horn to keep it in place. With her left hand under the horn, and taking a deep breath, she placed the cantle in her right hand and lifted the saddle in front of her for the trek to the stall. Smiling to herself, Lisa recalled how she had needed Paul to help her lift the saddle onto Clarity's back only a year earlier. Now she could do it all by herself.

Standing the saddle on its horn by the stall front, Lisa entered Clarity's stall. Checking once more that nothing was on his back, she laid the pad in place. He was finishing the last few bites of his hay that were scattered around the stall floor.

"Now stand still, boy, and no shaking!" Lisa commanded.

Clarity had been known to have quite a sense of humor, often shaking the pad to the ground just as she went to pick up the heavy saddle. This morning, however, he stood quietly for her. Retrieving the saddle, Lisa returned to the stall with the heavy load. She took another deep breath and hefted the saddle up into place onto his broad back, just behind his withers.

"There," she said in pride. "The hardest part is done!" Walking around to his off side, she lowered the stirrup down from the horn and laid the cinch against his side. Returning to his left side, she reached underneath to find the cinch ring and feed the latigo through the loops. In a flash, she had him saddled. As usual with his mischievous sense of humor, Clarity had taken a deep breath, expanding his ribcage and holding it. Once she was done, he would let the breath out and the cinch would be too loose. Knowing his antics, Lisa understood that she would need to tighten the cinch once more before mounting.

Next came his bridle. Taking the lead rope and opening his gate, Lisa led Clarity from his stall and into the barn aisle, closing the stall door behind them. She removed the halter from his nose and re-buckled it around his neck. Then she lifted the bridle to his forelock with her right hand and gently offered the sweet metal bit to his mouth with her left. Lisa placed her left thumb at the side of his wet mouth. This was the space in his jaw where she knew that he, like all horses, did not have teeth. Clarity opened up to accept the bit and then finished chewing his last few morsels of hay. Lisa wondered why the cowboys called the dark brown metal of the mouthpiece "sweet" metal. Clarity did not behave as if it was sweet tasting at all.

Clarity was cooperative about being bridled and lowered his head to make it easier for her small stature to accomplish. Lisa was only five feet tall and bridling Clarity would have been difficult without his cooperation. She unbuckled the halter from his neck and fastened it to his stall front where Paul liked them to be hung. Because keeping the barn neat was important to Paul, it had become important to Lisa, too.

Clarity jogged alongside Lisa, tossing his head left and right. He seemed to be looking forward to their ride as much as she was. Heading for the mounting block, they were both excited to get under way. Lisa strapped her insulated lunch bag over the front horn of the saddle. It held her journal, a pen, her lunch, and some treats for Clarity. Her leather bota bag was already filled with fresh water. The bag, bought on a trip to Mexico, had been a gift from her cousin. She slung it over the horn on the opposite side. Lisa buckled her daypack onto Clarity's breast collar. It contained the note she had written and a few other necessities for their ride. After strapping her jacket and rain slicker onto the back cantle of the saddle and donning her visor, Lisa checked to be sure that she had all she needed. Then she stepped up onto the block to mount Clarity, tightened his cinch, and climbed aboard.

"Hallelujah! It's Saturday, Clarity. Let's ride!" said Lisa.

Her mount shook his head, as if agreeing with her. Lisa never understood why her parents believed her time with Clarity should come last on her schedule. In their eyes, her homework, chores and time spent visiting relatives always came first. What was important to Lisa was pretty much in the complete opposite order.

But it was a precious Saturday and her parents were away. Her grandmother understood how important her time with Clarity was and granted her all the freedom she needed. She and Clarity had the entire day ahead of them to explore. She planned to make the most of it.

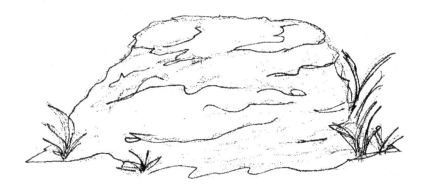

CHAPTER THREE

*C*larity felt really fresh and maybe too eager for a ride. Lisa decided to take him into the farm arena for a light workout before they went out onto the trail. He was in such good shape and Lisa had learned that when he felt fresh, it was better to let him work out his enthusiasm in the sand arena. She jogged for a few loops around the arena rail and then went into a soft lope until Clarity began to lower his head, telling her he was feeling calm and warm.

Walking to the arena gate, Lisa saw Paul heading for the barn to feed the other horses. She waved and yelled, "Thank you for putting his feed out, Paul."

"You're welcome. Have a fun ride, Lisa. Stay safe, okay?"

"Yep," she hollered back. "We will."

Her first destination was the large road loop that ran the farm's perimeter. It was where they often rode after lessons with her girlfriends and their mounts, or when they only had an hour after school to ride. Today they would not make the full circle, but instead go out the north side gate and explore the forest road. Clarity broke into a soft jog at Lisa's request.

The last cutting of alfalfa was taking place and Lisa hoped the farm would be lucky enough to get one more crop baled before a late fall rain or an early winter snow came. She loved the smell of the freshly cut field. Leaves were already falling, creating carpets of color on the ground. And the grasses were beginning to turn a softer green.

Approaching the broodmares' pasture, Lisa saw the lead mare of the band raise her head. The mares stayed outside all year, except when they came into the barn to foal. Paul had a special row of stalls for them with a huge sign that said Mare-ternity Ward. It took almost a year for each foal to develop. Lisa loved seeing how glossy and pretty each mare was when growing a big belly with the little treasure inside.

"Well," Lisa called out to the band of mares, "you are all looking healthy and wonderful, aren't you?"

Some of the mares raised their heads in acknowledgment. A few nickered to Clarity, who nickered back softly. Mostly, they were content to keep grazing as Lisa and Clarity jogged by.

Looking ahead, Lisa settled deeper into her saddle. She was breathing deeper, too, as she tried to push down the touch of fear she was feeling. From experience, Lisa knew the next pasture was a true challenge. As she followed along the farm's white fence line, she looked ahead at the band of yearlings on the far side of their own five-acre pasture. Living like little gang members on a Los Angeles street, they were unpredictable at best, usually bored, and looking for any excuse to cause some trouble. Sure enough, when one of the colts saw Clarity coming up the path, he called to the whole gang of fourteen yearlings, urging them to race over to the fence as fast as they could.

"Uh, oh, here they come, Clarity," Lisa said. "Now, come on, be a good boy, and remember I'm up here, okay?"

The yearlings ran as fast as they could toward them, bucking, snorting and kicking out at each other, acting wilder than wild. Lisa knew it was all Clarity could do to contain himself from also acting like a yearling as they approached. His ears were pricked forward and his head was raised high. Eyes wild, his tail flying out behind him, Clarity's jog suddenly became a fancy prancing dance.

Sliding to a stop, just inches before breaking through the fence, the colts and fillies were full of glee and mischief, snorting loudly when they saw Clarity. Lisa permitted Clarity to approach the fence line because he seemed to want to meet the yearlings nose to nose. Their little mouths sprang open, as if rudely smacking on big wads of bubble gum. Lisa knew this was an act of respect due her older mount. She could relax.

When the ritual of respect was complete, she touched Clarity with her boot heels, asking him to return to the pathway. He obeyed and the young colts and fillies trotted alongside them until their pasture fence held them back. Once more, they exploded in boundless energy, running and playing together all over their pasture. As Lisa and Clarity left their boundary, Lisa breathed a sigh of relief. Clarity held his head high, proud of his stature as a mentor to the young ones.

The farm path continued past the many pastures. Up ahead, Lisa saw the wooden bridge that spanned Magic Creek. Patting Clarity on the neck as he jogged over it like her Steady Eddie, they both swelled with pride. A year earlier, Clarity had been worried about the hollow sound of his hooves on the bridge and had become hard for her to handle. Lisa had asked Paul to ride him over it a few times so he would become used to the sound. Now he took the bridge effortlessly.

The two trailhead gates were just ahead. The one to the left was familiar to her because they had ridden the path many times. The gateway to the right opened to a path that went much farther. Rarely did they have the time or the permission to follow it. But this was a special adventure day and Lisa knew the gate to the right was the way to go.

Leaning over as far as she could from her saddle, Lisa could not quite reach the gate's clasp from Clarity's back. She also saw that even if she could unlock the clasp, she would not be able to reach the chain that kept it locked. Spying a large flat rock on the other side, she saw that if she dismounted and opened the gate, she could use the rock as a mounting block to remount on the other side. Lisa had been working on teaching Clarity a trick. He was learning to kneel for her so she could mount, but he had not quite mastered the cue. She was relieved to have a large rock as a handy mounting block.

Lisa climbed down from Clarity, passed the leather reins over his head, and led him to the gate. Carefully, she unclasped the chain and unlocked the gate, opening it wide enough for Clarity to pass through safely.

On the other side, Clarity bent down to steal a few bites of weeds and grass while Lisa relocked the gate and carefully threaded the chain back around the post, making sure it was locked as she had found it. The gate was a little sticky and not working the way it should. Lisa made a mental note to tell Paul about it when she returned from their ride. She knew he would want to know about that sort of thing before winter set in to stay.

Leading Clarity to the large rock, she asked him to stand still as she stepped up onto the natural mounting block. Putting her left boot into the stirrup, then swinging her leg over Clarity's back, she was like a ballerina landing softly in the seat of the saddle. She knew that Clarity adored the way she sat down on him so gently.

Lisa noticed a fog-like cloud floating along the ground in the distance. Clarity had noticed it too and had raised his handsome head to get a better view. Full of curiosity about the approaching vision, he was transfixed. Lisa leaned forward on his neck, using his ears like a site on a rifle barrel to line up the view ahead. The mysterious cloud seemed to be floating closer and Lisa had begun to see the shape of some being inside the foggy mist.

"Maybe we better go, Clarity," she said nervously, while squeezing her heels into Clarity's side.

Clarity did not move and although he was on full alert, he did not seem at all fearful or prepared to bolt. In fact, he seemed mesmerized. Lisa knew that if he refused to move, there was not much she could do. Yet, she felt a sense of trust that he would not allow anything to harm her. So she sat still, peering with her friend at the cloud-like shape.

The mists began to take form and shape, slowly materializing into the most beautiful woman Lisa had ever seen. She was clearly in focus to Lisa, but she seemed to exist within the cloudy mist, as if half within the world and half apart from it. Beyond human beauty, the being was more like a queen . . . or a goddess. Yes, that was it. She was a goddess.

She had translucent skin and a grace in her movements that Lisa had never seen, even on a ballet stage. Her slippers never touched the earth as she seemed to float towards Lisa. Her long, slender fingers were bejeweled and the tresses of her hair lay in long thick curls to her waist. Her waist seemed so tiny that Lisa thought she could encircle it with her two small hands. Yet her body was full of curves, like those of Lisa's mother.

The waistband of her gown sparkled from rich amethyst stones that matched her hair band. The gown looked like something Lisa would expect a royal queen to wear. It had layers of tulle and satin with brocade at the edges. Lisa was curious how she managed to float so airily with all of that woven cloth on her body.

Still, there was something indefinable about her countenance that made Lisa certain this woman was neither witch nor angel, nor was she mere royalty. Far above either, she seemed sent from the heavens—a goddess. Lisa pulled herself from her thoughts and looked straight into the eyes of the woman before her.

Speaking softly, the goddess said, "That is correct, Lisa. Your thought is correct. I bring no harm to you, child. I am Epona, the Goddess of All Horses. I summoned you here today, Lisa, for a very special commission. My request, on behalf of all horses, is that you and Clarity accept my commission to travel on a special journey. If you accept, my blessing will transform each of you. You will be riding as the Fairy Eponalisa upon the great stallion Wisdom. For centuries, others have performed this mission for me. This morning, I am here to request that the two of you follow in the steps of the many who have gone before you.

"I promise that if you are back promptly when you are finished, I will meet you here at the mounting rock by the gate. I will transform you back into the twelve-year-old Lisa, who lives on the other side of the golf course, and who must return home before dark to avoid worrying her grandmother. And Wisdom will be transformed back into your trusting mount, Clarity. Although you may feel that time and place have warped on your journey it will, in fact, be this very same day when you return."

Lisa was speechless, listening intently as Epona continued.

"You see, Lisa, there are many horses in the world who are bred and raised knowing precisely who they are and what their life purpose is. Like a race horse who was born and bred to race, a draft horse born of generations who pulled the merchant wagons, or a cow horse who drives and protects the cattle, such a horse is certain of his individual Calling and what he is meant to perform here on earth.

"Yet there are others who feel somewhat lost. They long to find their life purpose, but are not sure how to do so. I hold the knowledge of each of their Callings. So often the Calling involves "being" a certain way rather than "doing" a specific thing, and this sometimes causes them doubt or confusion. It is Eponalisa's job to find these horses for me. And as the Fairy Eponalisa, you will place upon each of them a Pronouncement of their true nature and Calling. Then they have 'clarity,' if you will," Epona said, smiling at her own pun.

Continuing, the goddess added, "You will be given the insight and magic of a powerful fairy to do all that is needed. And Clarity will take on the powers of the great and magical horse, Wisdom. Together, you will journey far and wide, being called upon to employ bravery, honesty and generosity of heart."

Epona paused for several seconds, allowing Lisa to contemplate all that she had explained.

"Will you and Clarity ride for me and the equine realm on this day, Lisa?" Epona then asked.

Lisa could feel her heart pounding. She was sure she was not dreaming, as this was wilder and more vivid than any dream she had ever dreamt. Bravery, honesty and generosity of heart? A mission for all horses? Clarity's calmness factored into her decision.

Lisa hesitated and then began. "Well, Clarity, we had planned to have an adventure today. So I suppose this fits right into our plans, eh?"

Clarity nodded his beautiful head at that exact moment. Lisa took this as a sign that he agreed to accept the commission.

"Well, yes, Ma'am . . . rather, yes, Epona . . . I mean, Your Highness . . . your Goddessness . . . well, yes. We accept!"

As soon as Lisa spoke the words of agreement, a damp mist of deep purple dust bathed both her and Clarity. It felt almost like the time her dentist gave her that funny relaxing gas to smell while filling her cavity. It also felt that her body was being transformed in some way. It was an odd feeling, but not unpleasant, rather like fizzy bubbles inside of her.

When Lisa became clear again, she knew she had become the beautiful Fairy Eponalisa, aboard the majestic Wisdom. She felt older and wiser than her usual self, self-assured and self-contained. Glancing at her dress's folds of rich fabric, her sparkling nails, the sequined slippers on her feet, and her newfound figure, Lisa knew that she had, in fact, taken on the full countenance of Eponalisa. Her thoughts began to gently slip away from the self she knew as Lisa as she became more focused on her task. Her last awareness of herself as Lisa was a feeling of complete awe at the breadth and beauty of her mount, Wisdom.

CHAPTER FOUR

There was the sound of a twig snapping as Grey Squirrel scampered down the massive tree trunk for a better seat. Eponalisa was due to appear on the horizon any minute and he was determined to see her up close this time. The last few times the fairy had ridden her route on the forest trail, Grey Squirrel had been working or sleeping. He had been disappointed to miss her ride.

Calculating in his tiny head, Grey Squirrel counted aloud to himself. "Thirty-foot tree, five main limbs, fifty branches. That is, uh, five hundred twigs and five thousand leaves!" Feeling truly grateful, he said to himself, "What a great home!"

The forest was restless, a restlessness that created a buzz of anticipation. All of Grey Squirrel's friends were also awaiting the fairy's appearance. Eponalisa rode through this section of forest only once a year. It was said that as she rode by, a sparkling silver and lavender fairy dust trailed after her that blessed all who were bathed in it. Grey Squirrel wanted a blessing from the great fairy this year.

Eponalisa carried the special mandate given to her by her mentor, the Goddess of All Horses, Epona.

The goddess had empowered the Fairy Eponalisa to bestow her blessing on horses—including the blessing of knowing one's soul purpose and life Calling. She blessed wild horses, fairy horses, massive draft work horses, competition horses shown by humans, ponies, miniature horses, loving farm horses, trail riding horses, carriage horses, circus horses and all other equines.

Grey Squirrel's grandfather had told him stories of the fairy's work. He had said that from the time when foals are born and stand on wobbly legs, most know and follow their Calling. A few, however, do not have this knowledge and search for it the majority of their lives as they learn life's many lessons. They yearn to discover the work they were born to accomplish. They search until one day, if they are lucky, they are each visited by the Fairy Eponalisa. Horses visited by the fairy receive the pronouncement of their true Calling, the work that sets them upon their path in life.

As a youngster, Grey Squirrel had wondered how the Fairy Eponalisa could know the life purpose of each horse. His grandfather had explained that she had been imbued with the knowledge by the Goddess Epona. As the Goddess of All Horses, Epona knew the true purpose of every horse on the planet. But while she was a "seer" who could see each horse's true Calling, she was not allowed to enter the World

Realm herself. She needed Eponalisa to tell the horses who were confused what their Callings were.

Grey Squirrel's grandfather had also confided that horses are all teachers and have much to share with humans. They provide enlightenment and lessons of truth. Humans need only open their hearts to the experience. Grey Squirrel respected this role, having had his own experience with just how difficult humans could be with squirrels. He was excited about seeing the fairy as she made her rounds to bless the horses and all other creatures with whom she came in contact.

Brown Forest Rabbit sighted the fairy and her horse, Wisdom, first. She set off a call chain among the smaller forest animals. Those who fly, those who scamper, those who burrow—all the forest animals passed the word along quickly that Eponalisa and her mighty steed, Wisdom, had been seen approaching the forest.

It was known to the forest animals that Wisdom's Calling was the mightiest Calling of all horses. He carried Eponalisa on her pronouncement journeys, serving her in love and light. He and the fairy each had a covenant with Spirit to protect the other. The two were inseparable.

As the flurry of chatter, screeches, chirps and squeaks spread throughout the open forest, Eponalisa and Wisdom steadily approached at a gallop. Wisdom and Eponalisa understood one another without the need for words. They each had the gift of clairaudience. Her thoughts passed to him and he listened to her through his finely tuned intuition. He obeyed her every wish with a trust born of knowingness that her wishes were always for the good of all.

From his strong, open gallop, Wisdom came to a long, smooth sliding stop. His haunches bent deep underneath him and his hooves made two lines in the earth as he slid to a stop. Now, after riding all night, they were finally at the very edge of new forest. Wisdom stood still and quiet as Eponalisa selected the first trail for the season's adventure. He wondered what direction they would take.

Part II:
The Pronouncements

CHAPTER FIVE

Eponalisa examined her choices and decided to travel up the small hill to the north. Wisdom caught her thought with his mind as soon as she came to that decision and moved off onto the north trail.

Wisdom's broad back and shoulders kept them both steady on the well-worn path that led along the side of the small hill and his broad hoofs stomped the dirt path into further submission. Meanwhile, Eponalisa rode gracefully aboard him. She held bejeweled leather reins in her small, slender hands and sat erect, perfectly balanced on Wisdom's back. Her luminescent wings fluttered lightly behind her, peeking out from the delicate, pastel lavender cloak that flowed in her wake. The cloak was as sheer as a dragonfly's wing. It seemed to spread a glow that emanated from her as she and Wisdom moved along the trail. Beneath the gossamer cloak, she wore a dress of deep purple velvet that seemed to flow with Wisdom's movement. For his part, Wisdom's every movement was regal. Together, there was magic and elegance to the pair. Like royalty, they rode into the dawn.

Eponalisa was filled with deep gratitude for Wisdom's loyal nature, steady gait, and enormous heart.

The autumn sunrise approached in full bloom, like a poppy opening, radiating light and color above the hilltop. Eponalisa stretched her graceful back and gave her wings a gentle flutter.

It had been a long night's ride and the little fairy was ready for a pleasant nap before venturing onward. Together, she and Wisdom sought a soft resting spot on the forest floor. Both trusted that Mother Nature would provide for them. Soon they found a thick carpet of grass under a large shade tree whose leaves had begun to fall, creating a soft nest. A small, silver stream ran alongside the grassy patch, making it a perfectly manifested resting place for the beautiful fairy and her mighty steed.

Quietly, Wisdom stepped to the edge of the site and bowed deeply, his left foreleg stretched out before him. He lowered his head down to the flat of his knee, allowing Eponalisa an easy and gentle slide to the ground on his open shoulder. Her satin slippers touched upon the grass tenderly as her wings assisted her in the softest of fairy landings. She tugged the purple blanket from Wisdom's back and used the blanket to create a comfortable resting spot on the grass.

Nestled in a powder blue velvet riding pouch and buckled on Wisdom's breast collar was a silver chalice. Eponalisa pulled it from the pouch and stepped daintily to the stream's edge. First, bowing to the East, she honored the sunrise and expressed her gratitude for such a beautiful spot to rest. Before taking her drink from the tiny stream, she blessed it for all the water and nurturance it provided to the earth, to the animals and most specifically, to the horses.

Eponalisa called to Wisdom, who joined her at the stream. Dipping her chalice into the stream, she quenched her thirst with the crystal, cold water. Wisdom placed his forefeet in the stream and allowed the cool water to run over his hooves and pasterns. Then he lowered his head and took one huge swallow after another.

As Wisdom drank, he noticed that many little forest animals, fairies, and gnomes were peering out from behind the rocks and trees on the opposite bank of the stream. Each creature was taking in the sight of the beloved fairy and hoping for a touch of her fairy dust. Eponalisa took no apparent notice of them. Wisdom was used to the attention his mistress drew. Still, it always touched his heart that she was unaware of just how special she was to all those in the forest.

Wisdom's coat was covered with a lavender and silver cloud of Eponalisa's fairy dust. It puffed from his coat in little clouds as he shook his big head and massive neck. Once he began, the shake felt so good that he continued to shimmy along his back, all the way to his curly tail. Several little clouds of her fairy dust rode on a soft breeze across the stream, blessing all the forest creatures who lingered expectantly. They would now be blessed with good shelter, food and love for the coming winter months.

Having finished her drink, Eponalisa carefully placed her silver chalice back into the velvet pouch. She patted Wisdom's neck and took two small apples from her bag. Then she returned to her blanket on the grassy patch. Wisdom followed her, pausing only to have a grazing nibble of the ripe grass.

As Wisdom caught up to her, Eponalisa unbuckled the throat latch strap of his heavy bridle. Pulling the crown over his ears, she gently dropped the slobbered bit from his wet mouth, being careful to let him spit out the bit without bumping his teeth in the process.

She held out one of the small apples on her palm, offering it to Wisdom. Eponalisa smiled at his precision in taking it with his teeth. Wisdom crunched the apple with his powerful jaws, savoring all its juicy goodness. Eponalisa nibbled on her own apple as she watched him eat. Once they had finished their repast, Eponalisa gave her beloved horse a little kiss on his large, soft nose and told him she was ready for her nap. Like the true and loving fairy she was, she settled onto her blanket and fell quickly into a peaceful, worry-free sleep state. Wisdom settled nearby, nickered softly, then slumbered deeply, snoring softly.

CHAPTER SIX

S tretching after her brief rest, Eponalisa mounted Wisdom as he knelt for her. She felt fully rested, alert, and eager to resume her journey. Wisdom, refreshed as well, fell into a soft jog as they started up the trail.

Eponalisa was pondering how quiet the forest seemed when she spotted an elk path to her left. She laid her leg softly against Wisdom's broad right side, asking him to turn onto the path. Wisdom dropped to a careful walk, pricked his ears forward, and started down the new trail. The elk path led to an open meadow where Eponalisa sensed she would find her first candidate.

As they crested the ridge, Eponalisa saw that her instincts had been correct. She and Wisdom peered down from the ridge to find a lush, green meadow below. A small band of broodmares grazed there with their sweet weanlings by their sides. The alpha mare, Corrina, raised her lovely head, sensing that someone important was near. She was elated to see the fairy looking down at her.

Eponalisa knew Corrina well and was happy to see her looking robust and strong. Her owner, the rancher, had given her a year off from motherhood, so she had no foal in the pasture.

As Wisdom and Eponalisa made their way down the ridge, the fairy took delight in observing the weanlings. A small palomino filly was busily nursing. A two-month-old paint colt stood on the shady side of his mama's hip, resting. A group of older foals napped in the cool grass. Some were barely visible, lying down flat on their sides. Others were curled up, with only their tiny ears peeking above the tall foliage. Two strong weanling colts raced about, venturing far from their mothers' sides, playfully kicking out at each other. They were just beginning to explore their autonomy, which would become important later in the fall when all the foals would be weaned. Eponalisa loved observing their youthful exuberance.

As lead mare, Corrina signaled the herd, alerting them to Eponalisa's arrival. Each mare quickly called her foal to her side. Excitedly, the foals searched and found their mamas. To steady themselves and feel secure, they nursed a moment or two from their mothers' generous bounty, greedily sucking in gulps of milk and then looking about before grabbing another swallow. Summer had been kind to the rancher and the herd. Everyone looked healthy and strong.

Once they had gathered back in a band, at Corinna's urgent insistence, Eponalisa noticed a small sorrel mare on the edge of the herd. She was not the only mare in the band without a foal, and yet she caught Eponalisa's attention above all the rest.

Gently, the fairy tapped her heels twice against Wisdom's sides as she picked up the jeweled reins, making soft contact with the bit in his mouth. Wisdom began to jog down the hill and confidently out into the expansive meadow. He sensed his mistress had an insight for one of the mares and was proud to be bringing her to the herd.

Corrina called out to Wisdom and he nickered in response to his old friend. Approaching the grazing herd would not have been such a calm event had Corrina not been in charge. Her band trusted her implicitly to keep them safe. Having faith that whatever she commanded of them would always be to their highest good, they did whatever Corrina asked.

Eponalisa approached Corrina with respect. "You look well, Corrina! I am so happy to see you."

"Welcome, Your Highness," Corrina replied with pride and gratitude. "We are honored to have you visit us again this fall. How may I be of service to you?"

"Epona has commissioned a Calling upon one of your young mares, Corrina. I am here to make her Pronouncement. She is the small sorrel, just there," Eponalisa said, nodding towards the mare. "Can you introduce her to me?"

"Oh, yes, gladly," nickered Corrina. "Her name is Bridget. Our rancher brought her home from the Ft. Worth Breeder's Auction. She was proud to have been selected for the prominent sale. She was heavy in foal to a great paint stallion and was delighted to have been selected by our rancher. She was carrying her first foal. Somehow, a few weeks before birth time, the unborn colt twisted inside of her. The doctor said the umbilical cord twisted and . . . well . . . sadly, he died."

After a respectful pause, Corrina continued.

"Our rancher helped her throughout the painful delivery. It was heartbreaking for him and for Bridget. The little colt was bay and white—a real beauty. It took a few days for Bridget to accept that her young son was not a part of the herd. She has been so sad, Your Highness, and we are not sure what to do for her."

With that, Corrina sighed and hung her head a little lower, contemplating Bridget's recent ordeal.

"Thank you for sharing, Corrina. Allow me to see if I can help her make sense of it all. Will you call her over here for me, Corrina?" Eponalisa asked.

With a beautiful, melodious neigh to the young mare, Corrina called for Bridget to join her in front of Wisdom and the Fairy Eponalisa. Bridget could not believe that Corrina had called her name. She looked to her left and to her right, expecting someone else to be responding to Corrina.

The whole herd was abuzz with excitement, encouraging Bridget to move forth. They parted to allow timid Bridget to walk between them toward Corrina. The little sorrel mare had heard the folklore of the fairy and her work for the goddess. She knew a few horses who had been in Eponalisa's presence and even one who had received a Calling Pronouncement from her.

As she drew nearer, Bridget saw the sparkling, translucent wings on Eponalisa's back. The fairy's gown fluttered in the breeze. Bridget marveled at the jeweled bridle upon Wisdom's head and noted the prism effect of colors in his curly mane and tail. He was unlike any horse she had ever seen and Bridget was full of awe.

Corrina nickered encouragement to her and with that, Bridget stepped a little more quickly.

"Eponalisa is here to see you, Bridget. Step forward and accept the generous blessing she brings you."

Bridget felt her heart flutter. She knew that just being chosen was a high honor and that forevermore, her life was about to be changed. She placed each small hoof further forward and was warmed by the loving look in Wisdom's liquid brown eyes.

Bridget bowed on one knee before the beautiful fairy. Wisdom bowed as well, so his charge could slip down his massive shoulder to the pasture grass below them. Her slippers barely kissed the cool earth, as her delicate wings once again supported her dismount. She was so graceful that she appeared to Bridget to be floating towards her.

Not wanting to frighten the mare, Eponalisa raised her right palm slowly, then rested her tiny hand upon the white star on Bridget's forehead. Passing energy along to Bridget through her hand, she crooned to the mare about her natural beauty.

"Bridget," she said in a whisper, "your beauty comes from deep within you. I am here to honor your Calling, dear one, as you have been blessed with a great mission. Yours is the Calling of Nurturance. You came to this earth to teach others in both the equine and the human realms about the truth of nurturance. The sacrifice you have just made has taught you, and everyone around you, a great lesson about the fragility of life—about the importance of life itself," Eponalisa explained.

The rest of the herd watched intently and strained to hear what the fairy was saying to the young mare. But the fairy spoke so softly, they could only hear a voice like a murmur on the wind, and not the words.

They would have to wait, hoping that Bridget would later choose to share it herself.

Continuing, Eponalisa said, "It is vital to step forward to walk in faith, even when your heart is breaking and you are in pain. Trust that there is a greater good to come for you in the future. The son, who seemed to leave you before his time, was actually right on time for his own Calling. He has become the Angel of Nurturance and Protection for many foals to come."

Bridget lowered her head even further and listened intently. Her heart was a fusion of pain and pride as she heard Eponalisa explain her son's fateful Calling.

"He is ready when you are," she continued, "to work as your partner from the angelic realm in assisting many other mares' foals. He is also ready to help human horse keepers to be healthy, strong, patient and full of faith—especially those who are caring for little ones.

"You see, Bridget," Eponalisa said tenderly, "the Nurturance Calling is a significant one. You are charged with teaching and fostering the importance of tending to others with a caring heart. There is, however, a vital agreement you must make in accepting the Pronouncement."

"What is that?" Bridget asked timidly, almost afraid to hear what the fairy would say.

"Well, you see, Bridget, the most important part of accepting this Calling is that you must agree to always put caring for yourself first!" Eponalisa explained. "Do you have questions, Bridget?"

Bridget felt exhilarated and confused, all at once. Still, she managed to reply.

"Why, yes, I do have one thing I truly do not understand, Your Highness." Hesitantly continuing, she asked, "How can I focus on nurturing others, yet choose to nurture myself first? Isn't nurturing about giving and doing for others? Is it not selfish to put me first?" she persisted.

Eponalisa smiled at the tiny young red mare and explained.

"You see, Bridget, if you do not give to yourself, you will become depleted and have nothing to give to others. Then you will be unable to accomplish your Calling to its fullest. The energy within you will run out. If that happens, you will be unable to serve others in the extraordinary ways that are being asked of you.

"Therefore, dear one, in honor of the highest power we all serve, you must always find ways to give to yourself. In so doing, Spirit will keep you filled with the energy you need to live your mission. Only then will you truly be able to give without the need of any return from those you nurture. You will feel no resentment and you will feel neither drained nor tired. The important example you set will teach others to do the same."

Eponalisa stepped back.

"I think I understand," Bridget nickered softly.

"Good, dear one," Eponalisa affirmed. "You have made the great sacrifice, felt the sense of loss. And you have the knowingness of how precious our loved ones are to us. Now you will begin to see your son's passing as the greatest gift you have ever been given. When we look at the bigger picture of life, we often realize that the saddest day of our life actually may be regarded as the greatest day," Eponalisa whispered, revealing one of life's great secrets.

"Take great care of yourself and teach the other mares to do so as well by the model you provide," Eponalisa counseled. "In the journey of your Calling of Nurturance, be sure to include interactions with the human realm. You see, oftentimes, just being in the presence of a horse is part of how humans take care of themselves. It is a privileged time for many humans and our spirits help to restore and rejuvenate them."

Smiling now at Bridget, Eponalisa waved her graceful hand. "Now go forth, my dear Bridget, and walk in faith into your life's work."

Bridget felt a little wobbly on her legs as she turned to face the herd. As she returned to them, the herd watched in amazement when Eponalisa began to flutter her wings and float back up onto Wisdom's warm back.

Wisdom felt tenderness for her in his heart. What he had just witnessed created the warmth he now held as a soft, loving space on his back for the fairy to sit. Wisdom felt humble as he sent a loving farewell from his heart to Corrina. Then he turned back to the trail, full of anticipation for Eponalisa's next Pronouncement.

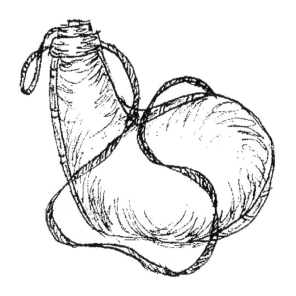

CHAPTER SEVEN

he warm rays of the late morning sun glistened
on Wisdom's coat. Eponalisa played with the
curls in his mane as they walked along the pathway.
She was deep in thought. Her legs swung loosely with
each step he took and her body was relaxed as she sat
centered upon his back.

A soft singsong of a breeze blew through the pine
trees. Wisdom wondered what Eponalisa was holding in her mind as thoughts. Experience had taught
him to be patient with her. She would move the
thoughts to her heart soon and then share them with
him in confidence. He kept his rhythm as steady as he
could, creating an almost hypnotic cadence as the
fairy continued to twist a soft strand of his mane. It
tickled a little and he twitched his shoulder muscles
in reflex.

The magical duo had walked the balance of the
morning in this way, covering a great deal of ground.
The terrain had changed and soon they stepped onto
the banks of a large irrigation canal. The canal seemed
to stretch all the way to the horizon. Eponalisa asked
Wisdom for a soft lope, hugging his sides with her
calves and lifting her seat lightly on his back. Her

thoughts had shifted and he could feel the intention in her request.

"Wisdom, we are headed for the farmland. We will follow the canal for a time, and then find a wonderful pasture where we can relax for the afternoon. Our next meeting is in the evening and we will need our rest," she informed him gently.

With that, Wisdom picked up the pace of his lope to a full gallop and fully enjoyed the cool air of fall in his lungs. Eponalisa's own curls blew back and her smile was filled with contentment. She loved it when Wisdom felt so free. He carried his head easily, with no need for any direction from her since the canal bank was straight and smooth.

They had covered some distance before the gallop once again became a lope. Finally, she sat back and he slipped back into a jog as he began to cool out. A light sweat broke through on his neck, cooling him further and proving the effort he had just expended. He felt wonderful and had enjoyed the run. Now he slowed to a walk.

Wisdom felt Eponalisa's light hands direct him to a narrow dirt trail off the side of the canal. It dove steeply down into a grassy pasture and he could feel his mistress lean back as he went down the slope. Large trees were spotty along the field's edge. They selected a very large one that would provide shade for the rest of the afternoon.

Coming to a stop under the large cottonwood tree they had chosen, Eponalisa slipped down from Wisdom's back. She threw her blanket upon the grass and unpacked her snacks. She had water left in her leather bota and a light repast in her pack. She found two cookies for Wisdom and, after unbridling him, she gifted him with the treats. He loved their molasses sweetness, gobbled them quickly, and headed towards the nearby cattle trough for a drink.

As her best friend was drinking his fill, Eponalisa looked around them and made a suggestion.

"This looks like a field the farmer has planted for harvest bales of alfalfa. I'm sure it's okay to rest here, but let's stay on the end row edge and not disrupt his crop."

Wisdom, too, had noticed how carefully the rows were planted. He saw, too, the straightness of the irrigation berms that separated each section and ran the entire length of the field. This was a farmer who took pride in his planting.

Grazing along the alfalfa field row end, Wisdom found plenty of sweet pasture. Alfalfa was to him like dark chocolate was to the fairy and he savored every bite. He kept his grazing to where the farmer turned the big machines to harvest the next row. No one had driven on it since the last harvest and it was a true treat.

Looking back from far down the field row, Wisdom could see Eponalisa sitting upright in a cross-legged position on her blanket under the massive tree. He knew she was not asleep, yet her eyes were closed. She was often completely still like this for several minutes at a time, sitting upon the earth as if drawing strength into her own roots from the damp ground. She seemed to be in a state of imagining, feeling the tree roots, which were steady and deep in the rich earth. After moments like this, when Eponalisa finally opened her eyes, they looked to Wisdom as if they had been recharged. He loved her so.

Eponalisa finally opened her eyes, stood, and began searching through her supplies for Wisdom's grooming tools. He was grazing his way back to her, feeling full and content.

"Wisdom, I think we should camp here for the night and start back out early in the morning. Will you stay here with me to rest? You put in a full day today, my friend," Eponalisa crooned as she began to take her dandy brush to his lustrous coat.

When she had finished, he stretched his right hind leg out behind him, balancing for a moment like a pro on three legs. Yawning in agreement, her faithful friend put his head down to find a soft spot to roll and settle for the night near her.

Eponalisa moved her blanket inside the curl of his large body to snuggle against him. There she rested, warm and protected. As she thanked him for the wonderful day, she could feel his heart beat a little faster. They shared and chatted easily and he appreciated how precious these moments with the fairy truly were.

The perfect circle of the full moon rose over the field's horizon. It had a brilliant glow. The face of the man on the moon was distinct and clearly watched over them.

"Oh, my goodness, Wisdom," Eponalisa teased. "The moon is so bright tonight, it looks as if someone put new batteries in it!"

Wisdom smiled at her positive thoughts. He had just been thinking to himself that it was so bright the coyotes would howl, making for a noisy night.

"This full moon in the fall, Wisdom, reminds us of all that we have," Eponalisa mused. "It is a moon of abundance. As it grows all the way to its fullness over the next few days, we will take inventory of everything for which we are grateful and what we want to invite into our lives. Let's sleep on that thought tonight," Eponalisa said through a tiny, pixie-like yawn.

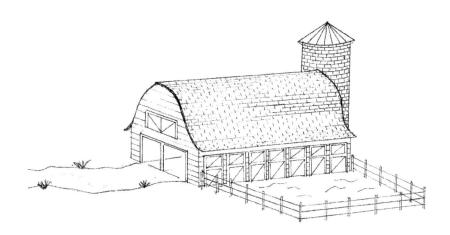

CHAPTER EIGHT

The morning came swiftly and Wisdom was eager for the day's adventure with the fairy. After freshening themselves with a splash and a drink of water, they were off on the farm road at the end of the field.

As they approached the farm, Wisdom could see a red barn on the horizon. A few horses were out grazing in a small fenced pasture. Other horses were saddled and resting at a hitching post in front of the barn, while others were hanging their heads out over their box stall gates.

Tail wagging and eyes bright, a small Golden Retriever trotted down the lane to greet the magical duo. Recognizing them as he drew nearer to Eponalisa, the small farm dog stopped and stared, never uttering a bark. As if speechless, he just stood and gave his tail a mighty workout.

Eponalisa pulled delicately on the reins, directing Wisdom to pause on the farm road.

"Well, hello there," she called to the dog. "What might your name be?"

Swallowing first, he barked out proudly. "Why, Toasty . . . th . . . tha . . . tha . . . that is my name," he stuttered. "Ga . . . ga . . . ga . . . given to me by my master's daughter when she was only two!" he added proudly.

"What a great name, Toasty. We are here to see Jeremiah. Do you know him?" Eponalisa asked politely.

"Do I kna . . . kna . . . kna . . . know him? Why, of course. He is the biggest guy on the place! Would you like me to ta . . . ta . . . ta . . . take you to him?" he offered.

"Why, yes, Toasty, if you will please," Eponalisa replied, appreciating Toasty's hospitality.

Wisdom walked a few paces behind the young retriever as he led them directly to a large pasture next to his master's home. Standing in the pasture, all alone, was the huge Belgium Draft gelding, Jeremiah. Grazing with his large round bottom toward the fence, he did not hear them approach until they were very close. Finally, and very slowly, he raised his huge head. After contemplating whether it was worth the effort to move, he gathered himself up and turned to face them as they approached.

As they came even closer to the fence line, Wisdom noticed that Jeremiah's hooves were the size of large feed dishes. He also observed how slowly Jeremiah moved toward them. Stopping a good ten feet back from the fence, Jeremiah awkwardly bowed on one knee, in full tribute to the fairy. It seemed quite an effort to raise his large head as he stood again.

"I am honored," Jeremiah nickered.

Eponalisa smiled. Her heart warmed at the harmonious vibrations coming from the large horse as she said to him, "Jeremiah, I have come to pay you a special visit. I am here, at the wishes of the Goddess Epona, to give you your Pronouncement. You have been a steady and great workmate for the farmer here," Eponalisa explained. "You have always been dependable and yet, also so gentle to everyone who works around you."

Wisdom sidled next to the fence and stood quietly. Eponalisa removed her long purple cloak and carefully draped it across his broad back. This made it easier for her to slide from his warm back to the top of the fence, stretch her wings, and float down to the ground.

Toasty became so excited at the sight that an almost involuntary bark escaped from his mouth while his tail wagged furiously. He had not seen anything on the farm this exciting . . . ever!

Eponalisa looked tiny and delicate at the foot of the giant Belgian. When he lowered his head to see her more clearly, his head seemed to dwarf her.

"Dearest Jeremiah," she began, "I have brought you a Calling from the Goddess Epona. Your Calling touches me deeply. I am here to place upon you the

Calling of Teamwork. Furthermore, this is bestowed upon you at a very special time, as I will explain today.

She paused for a moment, allowing Jeremiah to absorb what she had just said. Then she continued.

"Jeremiah, you have learned many lessons that prepare you for this day. You have learned to work well in tandem when your task is at hand. You have learned to pull your share and to move in a joint direction, not just your own. Often you have borne the load to allow your partner, whether equine or human, to rest."

Again, she paused for a moment.

"At times," she continued, "you were challenged to learn an even more important lesson. That lesson was the importance of knowing when to allow your partner to carry the load for a time, so you could rest. The Goddess Epona watched as you struggled and finally mastered that lesson, too," Eponalisa added, smiling.

"Now you work side by side with others, needing neither submission nor control. You allow the direction, pace and mutual energy to emerge. It is magnificent to witness. There is a force guiding your partnerships to the benefit of you both," she said.

This time, her pause was longer. She wanted to give Jeremiah the time to contemplate all that she had said.

Finally, she asked, "Does this make sense to you Jeremiah?"

When Jeremiah spoke, it was the slow and thoughtful speech of a horse who had experienced much and learned much from that experience.

"Why, uh, yes, Ms. Eponalisa . . . your Highness. I am in my midlife now and I have learned all that you say. I have had many great partners in harness. And I have been blessed to have a relationship with the farmer that is one of mutual respect."

Almost as an afterthought, Jeremiah then added, "I can feel his gratitude for my part when we work together to produce the crops that feed both his realm and my own. It is important work and I enjoy making the contribution."

"It is all so good, Jeremiah," the fairy assured him. "You work for your own goodness and the goodness of others, which makes the blessing for the highest good. Jeremiah," she explained, "the great Goddess Epona has asked me to make your Pronouncement at this time because you have a special understanding that will be needed in the months to come. Your farmer, whom you love, has a young daughter who has become very ill. She will be in her bed for many months and is very weak. He yearns to stay by her side night and day, but, alas, knows he must work and continue to farm. You see, Jeremiah, he has always been very focused in the past. He has always been able to fulfill his share of the duties you both handle. Now he is distracted and sad. He moves with a heavy heart. Your Calling at this time requires you to be ready to pull. Do you understand?"

Jeremiah hung his head even lower. Even from the paddock, he could feel the sadness of the farmer in his home. He had seen the farmer's little daughter many times as she rode her pony around the farm and played with Toasty. Eponalisa waited patiently for him to take it all in.

"What can I do to help them?" Jeremiah asked. "I want to do the right thing by them. Without my asking, he has always done the right thing by me."

The fairy smiled and explained.

"At times in your life, Jeremiah, you have had to push forward and you have been known to create the energy to make things happen or push them through. At this special time, however, you are being asked to pull and not to push. You will use your tremendous strength and move forward at a steady pace. Your farmer needs you to take the load while he is unable to do as much as he has previously. With your added might, he will be able to rest a bit and fill his heart with purpose, controlling what he can. Sadly, he cannot control what is happening with his daughter," Eponalisa shared.

"You see, Jeremiah," she said, "instead of making things happen, you are being asked to allow life to flow and to unfold before you as you move ahead in strength and steadiness."

Jeremiah bowed his head even further, almost touching his large hooves. He understood. Although his heart was breaking for his friend, the farmer, he was fully willing to serve. After a few moments of contemplation, he gently raised his head. Through his large, soft eyes, Eponalisa could see into his illuminated soul. A green healing light flowed from her heart into his eyes, filling his soul.

She crooned, "Breathe deeply, Jeremiah. Feel the difference as you take up the slack and quietly move into the next chapter of your Calling. You are a magnificent being and I am proud to have met you."

Eponalisa reached into her left pocket and withdrew two sugar cubes that had been infused with essential extracts that would allow him to have extra strength and energy. She offered them to Jeremiah from the flattened palm of her hand. His lips never touched her delicate skin, but using his whiskers as sensors, he slowly pulled the two cubes into his mouth with his lips. Then he chomped the small, yet mighty, treat.

Wisdom looked over at Toasty, who was lying down and resting his head upon his front paws. His tail was still wagging slowly, but the look in his eyes had changed. Toasty knew that he, too, needed to be all he could be for their farmer during this difficult time. He was grateful to have the information, as well as the deeper understanding.

Eponalisa glanced over her shoulder at Wisdom and saw him staring at Toasty. Feeling the loyal dog's concern, she addressed the sweet retriever.

"Toasty, do you hold a question for me?" the fairy asked.

"Um, well, I . . . I . . . I . . . I," Toasty stammered, "was wondering if you knew a . . . a . . . a . . . about whether my master's daughter will be well again one day." His golden head moved back down to rest upon his paws.

"Toasty, love and faith are the best healers of all. The farmer and his daughter are fortunate to be surrounded by their loving human and animal families. The outcome truly is not as important as the journey. Dear one, the answer will unfold in Divine time and it will be the best for all concerned. For now, Toasty, it is all about service, love, and faith."

Toasty then took a silent vow to himself to be the best he could be for the farmer and his daughter. He would keep a protective eye on the property and when the farmer needed it, he would be sure to let him know how much he loved him.

Eponalisa fluttered back up to the fence railing, balancing like a ballerina. She then slipped her leg over Wisdom's back and settled back onto him, feeling his warmth and receiving his vibration of love for her. As she pulled her velvet cloak on to comfort herself further, Wisdom knew she was holding in a few tears of her own. She had been touched by the love and devotion Jeremiah and Toasty had for their master.

As the beautiful Fairy waved good-bye, she added, "Remember, Jeremiah, he may not seem the same for awhile. Recognize that he is bearing a load, too, and trust that patience and love will see him through."

Eponalisa then guided Wisdom over to a small bulletin board on the outside of the red barn. Withdrawing a small yellow envelope with a note tucked inside, she carefully chose a blue pushpin and attached the message to the board.

"Our best to you all!" she called out.

Then she and Wisdom slowly retreated on the farm driveway. Toasty followed along behind until they reached the farm gate. He stood silently watching them, just as Jeremiah did, until the two were completely out of sight.

Wisdom continued to walk slowly, holding a steady pace, as his mistress did not seem to be in a hurry. He knew they would find a spot for an afternoon graze and maybe a chance for her to write.

Once they had settled in for a rest and graze, Eponalisa took out the leather journal. It felt large in the fairy's hands. She withdrew the pen and wrote a note to her human counterpart.

Dearest Lisa,

As you grow and mature, you may reflect back upon this journey and realize the truth of your own grace. Each part of this journey will leave behind a sacred piece of knowledge within you. These nuggets of understanding are for you to draw upon in life.

Perhaps our visit with Jeremiah will leave you with the gift of understanding the nature of Divine time. All answers, Lisa, will come to you when you need them and in the perfection of timing from the Divine. Allow the unfolding of knowledge and trust. You are in safekeeping.

Always with you,
Eponalisa

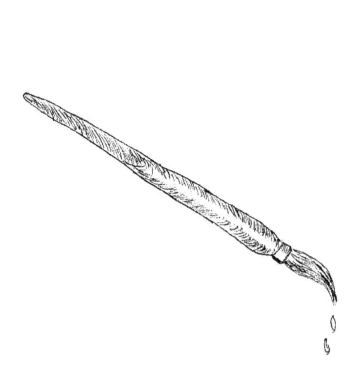

CHAPTER NINE

Refreshed and ready to resume her journey, Eponalisa stood and stretched. Both she and Wisdom had needed the time to contemplate. Their work together was joyful. But it also required both focus and compassionate communication with the horses they served. A nap now and then helped to restore them.

Eponalisa called to Wisdom and mounted, with the help of a nearby boulder. Then she stretched her wings and let them flutter back daintily. Holding the reins softly, she guided Wisdom back onto the trail, away from the farmland and toward the mountains. They rode silently as they traveled upward on a mountain trail, guided by the fairy's instincts.

They came to a rest at the top of the mountain. Breathing in the crisp, clear air, Eponalisa looked across an expanse of meadow that promised a lush treat for Wisdom and an inspiring setting for her next Pronouncement. She urged Wisdom down toward the meadow, but little urging was needed. He looked forward to an afternoon grazing snack and began a soft jog. Eponalisa centered herself gracefully to his beat, allowing her hips to sway to and fro.

Upon reaching the edge of the vast meadow, Wisdom lowered his head to grab a snack. He knew that winter would soon make this grass crusty and brown and found each promising bite tempting.

The sound of a small herd's hoofbeats could be heard reverberating on the mountainside. The herd was comprised of several horses that Eponalisa had met in journeys past. It was cared for by a local rancher who was allowed to pasture them on National Forest land.

The lead and alpha mare of the herd, Dancer, approached Wisdom swiftly, shaking her fiery head in greeting. Then she bowed down to Eponalisa on one knee, with confident brown eyes.

"Greetings, Dancer. Your herd mates look well," Eponalisa began, glancing up at her. "You have risen to your Calling as alpha mare quite wonderfully. I am so pleased for you. Dancer, Epona asked me to find you and meet the newest member of your herd. May I meet her?"

"Why, yes, Eponalisa, and welcome to the Snowbowl Meadow. We are all doing well, working to put on extra weight before the coming winter months. And, yes, we have welcomed a new mare to the herd. She has a filly by her side who is four months old and quite full of herself. The new mare carries the name

Sunny and wishes on the stars every night to know her Calling!"

"Dancer, please ask her to come and meet me in the middle of the Snowbowl Meadow. I would be pleased to greet her and share what Calling she holds," Eponalisa replied.

Eponalisa and Wisdom made their way into the center of the verdant meadow. The grass was so tall, it tickled Wisdom's belly as he grabbed mouthfuls of the lush treat. Long strands of grass hung out both sides of his mouth, while lime green foam began to form upon his white lips and muzzle. Eponalisa pulled off her slippers. The grass was so high, her toes touched its cool blades as her legs hung loosely from Wisdom's sides.

Eponalisa began to giggle as she watched Wisdom eat. He was enthusiastic but less than dignified.

"Wisdom," she teased, "be careful stuffing so much in your mouth at once, my friend! You may look like a glutton!"

Wisdom did not mind her teasing. He knew the fresh grass was a treat not often found on the forest trail and he was determined to take full advantage. He also knew that she understood this, too. Her teasing was more playful than serious.

Moments later, as Wisdom rose his powerful head, he saw a beautiful palomino mare at the meadow's edge with her foal. The mare seemed excited to join them, but her foal was not as confident about the wide, open space. The mare stopped every few strides to assure her foal, patiently allowing the baby to approach at her own pace. Never rushing her, the mare found ways to empower the little foal to find her own footsteps. She knew how to care for her offspring without undermining what her daughter thought of herself. The foal was still dependent on her mother's milk and only now forming her baby teeth. Still, when the foal reached down to taste the lush grass, her mother encouraged and praised her for her eagerness to explore new things. The mare saw her daughter as capable and courageous.

Sunny was unrushed as she led her foal to the fairy and her stallion. She pointed out which weeds to avoid eating and how to watch out for holes in the pasture made by prairie dogs. Sunny knew her daughter could trip or break a leg in one of the holes and cautioned her, teaching without hovering over the filly's every move. She counseled her how to watch for cougars and encouraged her to hold her head high and believe in herself.

"A cougar rarely picks on the confident ones," she told her.

When the little foal needed to stop and rest, the mare patiently sheltered her, allowing her to rest and nurse to calm her nerves. Even though Sunny was anxious to get to Eponalisa and Wisdom, she took her time. The best interests of her foal were her top priority.

In the herd, Sunny was also known to watch the elders and give them words of inspiration. She encouraged them to do what they could, but no more, on the hills and rough terrain. She often scratched their backs where they could not reach and found softer paths when the trail was too rocky for their feet. The elders all felt better about themselves because of the way Sunny spoke to them and honored their wisdom.

Approaching the special visitors, the mare kept her foal close to her side. They stopped in the field not far from Eponalisa and Wisdom. Sunny bowed low and deep. Her little one tried to mimic her, grabbing a tempting bite of a purple flower as she did. Sunny was in full wonderment of the famous fairy's magnificence. A soft breeze blew towards the mare, bringing with it the sweet lavender fairy dust that was floating in the air all around them.

On cue, Wisdom walked closer to the duo. Eponalisa studied the charming foal and praised Sunny for her remarkable young daughter.

"You have done well, Sunny. More than just healthy and strong, your daughter already has a wondrous spirit and vibration! She is confident and that is a reflection of your ability to teach while empowering her. Your daughter is precious. She walks in a state of innocence, where there is raw hope and trust. Her curiosity abounds as she ventures forth without fear.

"You, our dear Sunny, have the grand Calling of Protection. I have seen you honor the vulnerability of your own offspring, the youngsters of the herd, and the elders. You understand that vulnerability allows new experiences. Holding no thoughts of judgment, you teach others to find trust in themselves through learning, experiencing and true openness. The great Goddess Epona sent me here to place the Pronouncement of Protection upon you, Sunny."

Sunny's dark chocolate eyes appeared to double in size. She raised her head and began to breathe more fully into her broad chest, while listening carefully. She knew it was important to remember every word.

"You are being called upon to protect others—not physically, in battle, but in the way that comes so naturally to you. It is your gift, your Grace. Your protection of the others is essential and will call upon your courage."

Eponalisa paused to let Sunny digest what she was telling her.

Sunny was puzzled. She inquired, "Do you mean fight off the cougars? Or defend against the young stallions who attempt to dominate the herd?" Sunny hoped this was not what the fairy had in mind because she disliked fighting. "Is that what you mean?" she asked.

Eponalisa sensed the concern in the young mare's query.

"My dear one, you will protect without anger or judgment. You protect others through love, not fear. You will know the method. Boundaries must always be clear and your intense focus will often be in demand. Your gift of keen observation will be important. This is how you will protect."

Explaining further, Eponalisa said, "You will offer protection with love not defensiveness. I witnessed you doing this in your pathway to me today, Sunny. You have been given the rare ability to protect without controlling or demanding. You have been bestowed with the Grace of creating clear, clean protection. This Grace is supportive and does not restrain others or deprive them from learning their own lessons."

Sunny relaxed into the fairy's words. But she was unprepared for what the fairy said next.

"My dear Sunny, you are as a Guardian Angel and have gladly taken this role without reward or glory while here upon the Earth."

The light of truth and understanding filled Sunny's heart. She felt a golden glow emanate from her abdomen. A strength of will and determination filled her all the way to her backbone. Her heart felt strong and she had a new sense of herself. She reflected on all the times and ways in which she had carefully taught others in the herd what they needed to know to be safe. She pondered the many times she had championed them to believe in themselves and know their abilities. It felt joyous to know she was on the right path and had been following her Calling all along!

Not yet imbued with patience, her little filly was running in tight circles around her mother, kicking her heels up high above her head. Wisdom was not altogether sure the little one was ready to do these acrobatics as he watched her play. He nickered to her and she stopped in one quick step. Her little ears pricked forward, almost touching each other at the top. Cautiously, the little filly walked closer to Wisdom, her tail straight up in the air. She was clearly ready to run if he so much as blinked. Sunny and Eponalisa smiled. Their hearts were full of joy as they watched the little filly bravely approach the gentle giant.

Wisdom slowly bent his head down to meet her, being careful not to frighten her. He knew that her entire nose would fit in one of his nostrils!

"Good day, little one," Wisdom nickered so softly only she could hear him.

"Good day to you!" the little filly hollered back, shaking her head excitedly. "I know who you are. You are Wisdom, the Fairy Eponalisa's horse, right?"

Again softly, and with a filled heart, Wisdom answered, "You are right, little one. And what else have you heard about me?"

Stammering in excitement she yelled, "Well . . . well . . . well . . . I heard that you have the biggest heart of any horse ever never ever been borned!"

At that, Wisdom chuckled to himself. Fully enjoying their meeting, he felt his huge heart send white light to shower over the little precious one.

"I will see you again one day, when you are to receive your own Pronouncement. Until that time, listen to your mama and to Dancer," he counseled.

The little filly attempted to bow down to Wisdom on one tiny knee and, in a blink, almost completely lost her balance. In a flash, she regained her precarious steadiness. Collecting herself, she ran as fast as she could back to her mother, circling her with boundless foal energy.

Eponalisa brought her focus back to Sunny.

"Sunny, one more thing. The human realm needs your protection as well. Certain humans will come into your life, drawn to you for their own healing. You have the Grace to assist them in building their self-confidence, just as you do with your herd members.

You see, Sunny, we are all the same. They will be blessed by your patience and gifts to show each of them what is possible for them to feel, learn, and trust about themselves."

Feeling complete in explanation, Eponalisa returned to Wisdom's side and loosened a small pouch that was fastened to his jeweled breast collar. She floated back to the mare's side and carefully withdrew from it a tiny paintbrush and small, sparkling topaz stone. As Eponalisa touched the stone with her brush tip, it shimmered as if becoming liquid. A small amount of the gold color clung to the tip of the paintbrush.

She deftly raised her tiny hand to Sunny's face. The mare bowed her head lower to receive the mark to be placed upon her. The fairy carefully outlined the very edge of her white blaze with the precious topaz paint, blending it slightly with her palomino coloring. Sunny was being marked as an Earth Angel.

Tenderly, Eponalisa said, "Go forth and live in your Grace. Always know that the Goddess Epona is grateful to you for all you have done and will now do in the future. I hope to see you again."

With that, Eponalisa returned to Wisdom's side. She carefully cleaned the detail brush's tip and placed it back in the pouch with the gold vial of paint. Then she retied the small pouch back onto Wisdom's breast collar.

Wisdom bowed deeply, extending his left leg forward as far as possible so that Eponalisa could mount him easily. She settled her purple cloak about herself and drew her crystal scepter from beneath it. This she carried in her right hand, the jeweled rein in her left. With wings fully extended, she blessed the entire herd with her scepter and thanked Dancer for her care and great stewardship.

Wisdom turned on his haunches and began to jog back across the grassy meadow towards the trail. Reflecting for a moment, he forgot about the delicious, rich grass. A step or two later, the smell of the grass got his attention and he stopped to grab big gulps of the green treat. Soon the grass would be covered with snow. He knew also that they would be leaving the area soon and that he might not see this delicacy again for awhile.

Eponalisa allowed him a few minutes to enjoy the delicious grass, then urged him on. They had other adventures ahead of them, other horses they needed to visit. They rode along in silence, the silence of old friends who had just finished a bit of good and true work.

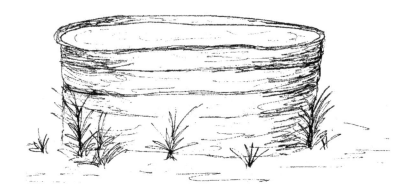

CHAPTER TEN

After stopping for a quick rest, allowing Wisdom a graze and Eponalisa a light lunch from her abundantly filled pack, the duo was ready to continue their journey. Leaving the lush meadowland, they climbed a dirt logging road deeply rutted from trucks that carried logs to the mill. The logging day began early and ended by early afternoon. By three, the loggers had left. Only the pungent smell of cut trees was left behind. Eponalisa noticed that this was a sustainable logging farm and was pleased to see that they had worked diligently to re-seed, plant and care for acres of young timber.

With sureness of foot, Wisdom fell into a soft lope at his mistress's request. His head was down, level with his shoulders, and his hooves cruised deftly alongside the road's ruts. After a few miles, the two were ready to slow their pace and take in the immense expanse before them.

Off to their left, Eponalisa saw their next assignment. She laid the right rein on Wisdom's neck and gave a little squeeze with her right calf to signal him to move left. She guided him carefully off the road and down to a corral fence below.

There, at the large round tank, Wisdom spied fresh water. Eponalisa freed him as he approached the tank and moved her left arm forward on his neck, releasing the reins so that his bit hung loosely on his tongue. With that movement, Wisdom could stretch his neck down and freely drink.

"Do you want me to drop the bridle, Wisdom?" she asked. Already happily drinking, he shook his head side to side to tell her it was not necessary. But he was touched by how caring she was.

As Wisdom barely took his last swallow, a horrendous racket inside a cloud of dusty chaos moved toward them at a rapid clip. The split rail fence would never hold the bunch of ruckus if they missed their estimation of its location.

Bucking, snorting, stumbling and almost laughing were four large, sweaty mules. Amazingly, they came to an abrupt stop just short of blowing through the tiny fence. A huge dust devil followed right behind them, passing through the fence and flowing toward Eponalisa. As it neared, however, it seemed to drift above her and float on past, touching neither the fairy nor Wisdom.

Eponalisa caught herself giggling aloud at the sight of the rough and tumble group. Wisdom raised his head, striking a proud posture, as he asked them for attention worthy of his famed mistress. One by one, the mules recognized who was in their midst. They bumped and bit into each other to get one another's attention.

Finally, the largest of the clan began.

"I beg your pardon. We just got off work and are known to cut up a bit in the cool of the evenings. Sorry Miss . . . Highness," he brayed.

Wisdom felt a slight burden of disgust. He might have found it humorous but for his sense of duty about the Mission. He relaxed only when Eponalisa burst out laughing. Her laughter told them that it was quite all right and that she thought they were wonderful in their play. She never ceased to amaze him.

Again the largest of the mules spoke.

"Allow me to introduce myself. Myself, well I am Rowdy, Miss. And these here fellas are my crew. This here's Rocky, and these are Earnest and Buck."

"Well, pleased to meet you, Rowdy. I am Eponalisa and this is Wisdom."

Rowdy quickly interrupted. "Oh, Miss, we do know who you are. The legend of Epona and her fairy helper is well known, even to the likes of us!"

"Well, Rowdy," she giggled, "you are on my route this fall."

"Me?" Rowdy brayed in disbelief. The others stomped on his hooves, shoved his hips, and nipped teasingly at his behind. The fairy could see it was all in good fun.

"Yes, Rowdy, you are," she continued. "I have a Pronouncement for you—your Calling if you will."

Rowdy felt nervous and somewhat embarrassed in front of his friends. He knew they would tease him unmercifully at work the next day. At the same time, he had secretly been hoping for an answer to the question he held deep within.

Eponalisa read his thoughts and spoke.

"It seems, Rowdy, that our Goddess Epona has heard your heart asking if you are being all you are meant to be with your life. She has heard your doubts and has understood you have them because you fill your life with so much fun. She knows you work very hard assisting the loggers with their very dangerous jobs. And she also knows you have fun while you are doing it . . . and every moment in between!"

Rowdy looked embarrassed again. His buddies continued to play disrespectfully. Tiring of their antics, he pinned his long ears flat against his neck and shoved his crew back a few steps. They knew he meant business, backed off, and stood bewildered. So quietly that it was almost a whisper, Rowdy admitted to the fairy that he did wonder about his life.

This time Eponalisa decided to remain on Wisdom's back to speak, deciding that this was her best and safest vantage point.

"Rowdy, you have been given the Calling of Camaraderie. Around you at this time is immense support and you are receiving comfort by being with others. Their support is important and it is understood that you will be somewhat dependent on them during this time as they are on you. Listen to their counsel and contribute your own viewpoint frequently.

"The task at hand in your journey, Rowdy, requires that you work with others. By doing so, you will discover the benefits of mutual contribution and interdependence before you go off on your own.

"Rowdy, those in the human realm watch as you and your crew are working as a close-knit team. They see the mirror of your camaraderie and it helps them work more as a team, having fun together, too."

Pausing, she then added, "True friendship can boost your thoughts, beliefs and feelings. Others may see and contribute to you what you are missing and, conversely, you will bring to the forefront what they may be missing. For now, Rowdy, enjoy the camaraderie!"

She smiled as Rowdy visibly relaxed with her words.

She continued. "The work you do is hard and often long. Your bright spirit keeps your crew and the human realm in good spirits with full hearts. Your Grace is an important one Rowdy. Do you understand what I have shared?"

Rowdy stood in silence, as if humbled by all that was shared. His crew was also eerily quiet and unsure what to say or do.

Rowdy finally brayed loudly, "So what you are saying is that I am free to feel the joy and humor I carry each day? In fact, it is how I am supposed to be?"

"Yes, Rowdy, you have it! It is a gift to everyone around you!"

Rowdy was bursting with pride and happiness as he clumsily bowed down to the fairy in appreciation. Eponalisa blew him a kiss that was accompanied by her lavender blessing dust. It floated gracefully to him and landed on his large muzzle. As Rowdy bowed, Rocky reached over and bit him on the behind while Buck nipped playfully at his knees. And soon the entire chaos of roughhouse had resumed. Rowdy solemnly nodded in thanks to Eponalisa and quickly joined the others. The group ran the length of the paddock in a cloud of dust, looking more like professional rugby players than a working team of mules.

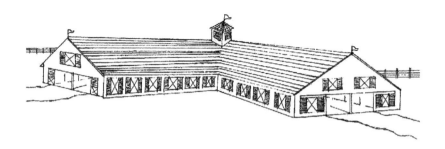

CHAPTER ELEVEN

S miling, Eponalisa and Wisdom watched the antics of the four mules for a minute and then turned to set out again. Feeling playful, Wisdom tossed his head and twisted his neck back and forth while Eponalisa played with his mane. She cued the magnificent horse into a lope as they reached the dirt logging road.

She could feel that his muscles were taut. He was eager to let loose and run. After placing her scepter safely in its sheath and settling deep in her seat, she leaned forward, squeezed with both legs, and released her steed for an all-out run.

Wisdom relished the gain in speed. He sensed that Eponalisa was perfectly balanced and safe upon his back and lengthened each stride. Wisdom stretched his neck. Nostrils flaring and mane flying as if on its own, he gained more and more speed every second. Eponalisa loved the thrill and freedom of it all. She leaned forward, placing her face closer to his neck to help maintain her center of gravity as he poured on more speed. His powerful legs carried them across the terrain swiftly, safely and in joy. The sound of his hoofbeats hitting the dirt, accelerating, echoed down the road.

The road gave them permission to gallop for a long way, changing from forestland to farmland again. They ran together, fully in the moment, breathing in the crisp air. Their surroundings became a blur of trees, road and grass. A raven swooped alongside them as if racing the incredible horse and playing in his draft. Keeping her wings safely tucked underneath her cloak, Eponalisa smiled inside as the raven flapped beside her.

When Wisdom's lungs began to burn, he brought down his speed. His mistress had never asked him to continue a gallop beyond his endurance. Instead, she partnered with him as he let himself expand and explode in the run. He shortened each stride, little by little, pulling the speed down to become more contained again. Eponalisa sat up slowly, keeping her balance in perfect alignment with his form.

After a few minutes, Wisdom had resumed his usual collected lope. A light sweat formed on his neck, curling his hair coat. Breathing hard and enjoying the feel of victory over his run, he slowed to a jog and finally came to a stop. Eponalisa felt his massive chest expanding with every breath. His heard pounded and his eyes flashed, excited and wild. Perking his small ears forward, he stared fixedly for a long time. Eponalisa always wondered if he was seeing into the "other world" when he was in this space.

After a few more minutes at rest, Wisdom's heart rate returned to normal and his nostrils softened. Both he and his mistress still felt exhilarated from their all-out run. Eponalisa suggested a slow walk along the new path.

"Thank you, Wisdom," Eponalisa crooned as she smoothed down each section of his mane. "You are more magnificent than Pegasus when you run like that. I feel so delighted to have been aboard!"

Wisdom knew he had not simply craved the free run, but had needed it. For him, it was a release, a joyful playfulness, a stretching of all that he was.

"You are most welcome, Your Highness. Because you are such a talented rider, we can do that together."

They walked along in silence for a few miles before spotting a perfect place for the night. When Eponalisa first spotted the large white barn at a distance, she thought how wonderful it would be for Wisdom to have a good night's rest in a bedded stall. She then realized it was the home of her next assignment and that there was a strong possibility they would manifest a place to stay there.

The sun was just about to sink below the horizon. The farm they approached was clearly a large, professional facility. It hulked in darkness, save for a few security lights. As they walked the pathway, they followed the white fencing that surrounded the pastures.

One large pasture seemed to go on forever with what Eponalisa recognized to be careful planting and maintenance so as not to be overgrazed. Several obstacles were deliberately built within the borders of the fence line. It was clearly built as a cross-country jump course. The first and smallest rectangle, fully crafted of stones and logs, was where the course began. Then jumps of all types of architecture were set all over the large acreage. Some of the jumps were made from large logs laid on their sides, making them each at least two feet tall. The approach to a few was uphill. Some were crafted of wooden boxes or even tarps or gates.

The trees in the paddock had all been respected and left in place during the design and construction of the course. Each obstacle sat at a differing height and angle. The ground approaching each jump varied from flat to downhill, and some were over the challenging water holes or creeks. Eponalisa marveled at the athleticism necessary for a horse and rider to maneuver the course.

After leaving the cross-country course's natural brown pole fence line, they rode along another type of fence line. This arena was enclosed by a four-foot concrete retaining wall that leaned outward at an angle. Two sets of stadium bleachers for spectators to perch upon framed the expansive arena on both sides.

The inside perimeter was a large expanse of ground. However, this time there was no grass in sight. Instead, it was manicured dirt mixed with just the right amount of sand so a horse would have the perfect footing and traction to clear the jumps. The tiny ruts of the arena's tractor drag showed it was well taken care of on a daily basis. Eponalisa knew that this type of maintenance was done to provide more safety for each horse and rider.

The stadium jumping arena was filled with freshly painted man-made jumps, each one crafted from wooden standards made from four-by-fours and round striped poles. Some were smartly designed to have the appearance of gates. Others, painted boxes, had been given a faux finish so they appeared to be stone walls. Some were set close together to be jumped in quick succession, while others were followed by colorful blue water boxes.

As Eponalisa rode on, she noted how challenging the course would be for a pair to execute.

She passed the dressage paddock next, appraising it as she silently rode by. It was framed with a neat white fence less than two feet tall. The fairy was familiar with the ballet-like moves the horses practiced in this ring. There were signs posted, very deliberately, with individual letters of the alphabet on them. These were dressage letters, posted to aid the riders in executing the precise maneuvers for which dressage was known. It was impossible to tell that riders had even ridden the ground that very afternoon. It all looked perfectly groomed, as if someone had just run the tractor and drag upon the soil.

The entire facility was truly a premier setting for horses who exhibited in what was called three-day eventing. It was one of the finest facilities of its type that Eponalisa had ever seen. She felt certain that this was the pristine location of her next assignments.

A low cloud cover obscured both the moon and stars. Eponalisa was glad for this natural occurrence because they could easily approach without being noticed. All the horses appeared to be snug in their stalls in the large show barns. Even the facility's dogs seemed to be missing. She sensed that the larger of the two barns was where she would meet up with the next chosen ones to receive their Pronouncements.

She reined Wisdom silently toward the barn, staying in the shadows as they approached. At the barn's end doors, Eponalisa dismounted silently. Tiptoeing, she snuck over to the huge rolling door. Taking a deep breath, she pulled as hard as she could on its handle. The mighty door slid on its rollers to the side.

Opening it just enough to allow Wisdom to walk through, she noted that the barn had a few low lights on. Horses began nickering at the sound of the door opening. She quickly asked them to remain quiet to avoid alerting the farmhands.

Eponalisa could tell by how well the grounds were manicured and how well cared for the horses appeared that the farm's crew was a diligent one. She did not want to cause anyone concern that night, as the human realm often did not understand things they had never seen. She and Wisdom definitely qualified as beings not seen by humans every day and she wanted to avoid creating a disturbance.

Amazed and in awe of who was entering their barn, the horses were all quick to obey her request. There were only a few excited whispers to their neighbors down the long row of stalls about their great fortune to have Eponalisa and the famed Wisdom in their barn.

It was such a rare occurrence to even have a sighting of the famed pair. But the fairy trailed magic dust as she came through the barn and every member of the herd knew that the great gift of the fairy's dust sprinkled through the barn would mean an abundant year of lush pastures, plentiful water, a bounty of new foals for the herd, and many other gifts for them all.

Eponalisa led Wisdom over to the bath rack and quickly un-tacked him, taking everything off so that he could enjoy his warm bath. After uncloaking herself, she turned on the warm water faucet and prepared to care for her best friend. Using her wings to gain some height, she held the hose and ran the warm water all over his body. The salty crust of sweat from the afternoon run melted away and streamed down the drain.

Wisdom felt indulged by the luxury of his bath and wished it would never end. But Eponalisa did not want to waste any water by using more than they needed for their task. She carefully turned the faucet off and placed the hose back on its hook. She then ran a comb through his mane and tail, braiding each. Before she could allow Wisdom to rest, she knew she must do a few more things in his care.

Eponalisa checked each of Wisdom's hooves to make sure he still had all of his shoes in place. She also examined his legs for any cuts or scrapes that would need tending. She was relieved to see that they had accomplished their playful all-out run without any price having been paid.

When she finished her caring routine, she turned to the large black Friesian stallion in his stall across the aisle. Most of the horses in the barn were Friesians with other warmbloods and thoroughbreds mixed into the herd. Eponalisa respectfully asked the stallion if there was an empty stall where she and Wisdom might rest for the night. She assured him that they would be gone before feeding time in the morning.

The stallion was clearly in charge. He said they were privileged to have the pair stay the night in his barn. He directed Eponalisa to the fourth stall on the near side. The horse who lived there was away at a horse show, along with several of the others.

After settling Wisdom into the stall, Eponalisa smiled as he lay down to roll and roll in the fresh, sweet sawdust. The sawdust had been thickly laid over the rubber stall mats, making a comfy haven for him to rest.

Eponalisa then returned to the Friesian stallion.

"May I trouble you a bit more?" she asked, only to find the black stallion bowing on one knee to her.

"Oh, Your Highness, you are most legendary in your kindness and could never be of any trouble to us. We have heard stories of the many fortunate ones who have found such peace in their hearts after receiving your Pronouncements from Epona," he neighed.

Eponalisa smiled. She felt so deeply grateful for her own Calling of helping others through Epona's Pronouncements. It was her Grace. She was proud to be serving horses in this manner as she executed her duties. It was an honor to represent the Goddess Epona and a pleasure to spread her love and caring.

"Thank you. You are so kind. I have been sent to this fine facility for two different horses. I must find them and work with them a bit so that we may be gone before sunup. But first, can you tell me a little more about this fine facility?" she queried.

The stallion puffed and expanded to what seemed twice his resting size.

"As the stallion of this farm, I pay close attention to all who come into the herd and any who leave. It is a huge job because we are a competition show barn and there is always some coming and going. The herd is always changing and it is my job to watch over all of them."

Continuing with his lecture, he informed her, "We are supremely cared for by the human realm, with little asked in return. We have the best of feed three times per day. We have soft, clean sawdust each night and large, private paddocks to play in. In the winter, we have blankets and heat in our barn and in the summer, we have fans to cool us. The ground we walk on is always freshly groomed for the best footing and our water bowls are scrubbed clean every day," he boasted.

With no pause he continued, "Each day we are bathed and groomed. Most days, we have our exercise time, so we can stay fit and able to fly over the jumps. On our favorite days, we are learning something new with our partners from the human realm. They are learning, too. And if it does not come easily, they usually take responsibility, trusting that we are doing our best."

He beamed with pride, finally adding, "If one of us has a sports injury, the best of care is provided, to assure we will recover quickly."

Eponalisa enjoyed the dignity with which he explained it all to her.

"And when you go to the horse shows?" she asked, prompting him further.

"Well," he neighed, "when we travel to the horse shows, we load into a large trailer that floats over the ground. It is pulled by a huge truck and several of us go at one time. We cover many more miles than we would want to run. We watch out the tiny windows and see the world pass by. It is truly very exciting! Once there, we are treated like royalty and meet many strangers from the human realm who praise us and tell us how beautiful we are."

Now the great stallion lowered his voice to a whisper and met her eye to eye. In a confessional tone he added, "In fact, Your Highness, it is hard to stay humble because we are applauded and praised so very much."

Eponalisa's heart warmed to the big stallion. She could feel his genuine pride and caring for all the horses in the barn. He radiated the very essence of protection and the accumulated knowledge that brings about sound judgment for the greater good.

"Oh, my dear friend, there's no need to worry about that at all. You are filling a special need for the human realm. You see, they often have a desire to exhibit beauty and it is special for them to team with a horse in the accomplishment of something that is both beautiful and athletic. I am so glad that you are revered in this way and remembered with gratitude," she assured him. "I pray it will always be so," she added pensively.

Too often, she had seen humans lose their appreciation for horses after they could no longer perform. She knew that humans had a lot of growing and learning to do before all horses would be so well cared for and with such gratitude.

"Please help me, if you can," she asked. "I am here to share with a horse who feels frightened and sad right now. It is because he is so far away from where he was born."

The stallion knew just who she was referring to.

"He is new here, imported from the Netherlands, which is our home country as *Friesan paards*." The stallion loved imparting lots of information and added, "He is said to have cost the human realm a great deal of money. He is our next great hope for the show circuit and they are concerned about his depression. He is in the last stall by the feed room. I am glad you are here to see him, Your Highness, for he is indeed sad. I am afraid we have not yet been able to find a way to comfort him."

With that, Eponalisa thanked the stallion and walked quietly down to the last stall. There, standing at the back of his stall against the wall, was one of the largest black horses she had ever seen. He was so black his coat looked almost blue, like polished steel. She cleared her throat and the tiny sound awakened the Friesian horse. When he saw her, he recognized her immediately. Looking as if he thought he must be dreaming, he stood speechless and frozen in space.

Eponalisa asked him in Dutch what his name was and he replied, "Albert." He was from a fine Friesian family in the Netherlands. He had been imported to the United States and felt quite lost. Eponalisa asked him to share the story of his journey and was quite taken aback when she heard it. Albert had been in transport for over forty-six hours. During that time, he had suffered a long airplane ride. He had also traveled in several different trailers and had stayed in many different facilities along the way.

Albert reported that he was trying to learn English but, alas, had not yet done so. He was lonely and he was frightened about what would be expected of him in the coming days.

Eponalisa felt a surge of compassion for Albert. She had listened to his story and now wanted to help him understand some things she thought would bring him comfort. She began to speak with him in his native tongue of Dutch. She had barely begun when he came over to her at the gate and asked if she would like to rest upon his back as they chatted. Fluttering her luminescent wings, she flew up to his back. It was so broad and flat that she lay down backwards resting her tiny head on his hip as she spoke.

"You see, Albert, the unknown and yet to be revealed are always a mystery to us. Recently, you have been trying to control the uncontrollable. You may have been seeking security, predictability, and all that feels certain and safe. But to live with everything revealed and certain creates a sacrifice that you must examine at this time."

"A sacrifice?" he asked, puzzled by what she had said.

"Why, yes, a sacrifice," Eponalisa assured him. "You see, pure certainty creates a life without adventure or passion. Your desire for all that is comfortable and safe is natural, yet at this time, you are being asked to take a risk. You are being asked to release your need to know all outcomes and become willing to trust," the fairy counseled.

Albert was attentive. Yet she could see he doubted his ability to do what she had asked.

Eponalisa patted Albert's side and told him, "Breathe. And with that breath, take in faith that some level of uncertainty will enrich your life more fully than you can even imagine! You see, Albert, your life can be fully charged only to the degree you can handle uncertainty."

She stopped, letting him consider it all.

The giant Friesian pondered what she had said. Eponalisa dozed upon his broad back as he thought about his situation from this perspective. Then she began to feel the huge horse breathe deeply, slowly filling his great lungs and expelling all fear. He took several deep, slow breaths. She could feel his back rise and expand more and more with each one.

When Eponalisa felt he was ready, she asked him carefully, "Albert? Are you prepared to hear about your Calling now? I have been sent to find you and pronounce your Life Calling on behalf of the great Goddess Epona, the Goddess of All Horses. I want to make sure you can hear me and are ready for the Pronouncement."

A large tear rolled down the big Friesian face. His heart was swollen in gratitude for her kindness and the new framing of his journey to America. Everything looked different to him now. It was as if the loneliness and fear had been replaced by excitement. And he knew he was ready to face his wondrous challenges!

As she watched the tears of gratitude roll down his cheeks, she felt tears leak from her eyes as well. The stall was filled with a soft lavender light. It was the light of knowingness, intuition, and understanding. She knew he was ready.

"Yes," Albert said, "I wish to hear my Calling and I promise to do my best to fulfill it."

"Wonderful, Albert," Eponalisa whispered. "You carry the Calling of Infinite Power. You are about to receive a magnificent vibration. I want you to close your beautiful eyes and envision a wheel of light about you. This circle of light showers upon you as you make your way through this next time period. From this creative space, as you become more aware of its benefits, you will be able to use all of your productive self. Love is filling your being, Albert. And you will now bask in the glow of its light."

The fairy was silent for a moment while Albert took in the vision. When he opened his eyes again, she continued.

"The human realm has brought you here to join this facility, and soon you will meet the young woman to whom you are a gift. She will learn much through you about herself and her own sense of confidence. Her heart is so ready to love you. She needs you as her trusted confidant. While her life is rich by monetary standards, it is poor when it comes to knowing and receiving love.

Albert nodded in compassion as Eponalisa spoke.

"The two of you will be lifelong partners. You will remain with her forever. Within your lifetime, her children will also ride upon your back. There are many life lessons she will learn through you. And she will be called on to share these lessons with others in a variety of ways when she becomes an adult. She will be one who assists the human realm to see horses in a different and healing light. It will be your work with her heart—far more than exhibition—that prepares her. Do you understand this?" Eponalisa asked.

The young Albert took in the information and could see the wheel of light spinning before his eyes, even now that they were open. Now his heart was swollen with gladness to be in this new land. He wondered how it came to be and Eponalisa sensed his query.

"You see, Albert, you must enjoy this part of your life's journey. It is well earned and it will balance some of the challenging times you experienced in the past. From this space, you can move forward in manifesting your own heart's desire. Seek to remember this feeling and time period so that you may draw upon it when challenges appear again in the future. Trust that joy will return to you many times in your life.

"You are given the Grace of Infinite Power. You are destined to teach others about their own infinite power. I entrust this Calling to you now, Albert."

The young horse experienced a deep sense of calm and sensed there was no need to reply. He stood still, as if reading the fairy's thoughts as they seemed to wander from him. Eponalisa felt compelled to once again pull out the leather journal and pen from the pouch on her shoulder. Considering for a moment what to say, she finally bent over the journal and wrote.

Dearest Lisa,

I trust that this nugget of truth will also be a wonderful lesson for you in the years to come. As you make your way to adulthood, you will face uncertainty about what your career will be. You will question how you will spend your life with horses.

We ask you to remember that uncertainty is what gives your life excitement and passion.

As with most young women, you, Lisa, are full of infinite power. You will manifest your own heart's true desire. By remaining true to your heart's desire Lisa, you will always make the correct choices.

Follow your inner knowledge of who you truly are, trusting yourself to make the right choices and holding the faith that those choices will ultimately be accepted as the correct ones for all those who love you. In love and light, Eponalisa

Albert felt the fairy nodding off after she finished writing and tucking the journal into her bag. She slept on his back and he felt honored to carefully hold her as she dozed. He could feel the love within her seep deeply into his spine and infuse his system with joy, love, and serenity.

CHAPTER TWELVE

Eponalisa awakened to the sound of Wisdom calling to her from his borrowed stall. He felt quite refreshed and wanted to lay eyes up his mistress. Eponalisa stretched before sitting upright and thanked her newest Friesian friend for gifting her with such a comfortable space in which to sleep. He seemed full of joy this morning and ready to greet his new Calling.

The sun was not yet up, but she knew it would not be long before the facility help arrived to begin their chores. Eponalisa quickly threw in some fresh hay for Wisdom to eat for breakfast. Then she walked the barn aisle in search of the other equine she needed to visit. As she approached the stall door of a fabulous bay mare, she knew she had found the correct soul. Deep red with a full lush black mane and tail, she was a true classic beauty.

The mare looked concerned about the fairy's visit and Eponalisa knew why instantly.

"Oh, my dear, I remember you," she said to the bay mare. "I met you years ago when I gave you Epona's Pronouncement. It was to always step up and carry forward, wasn't it? Isn't your name Lana?" she asked, as she brought back the memories.

The mare nodded and came closer to her stall front.

Eponalisa added, "I remember also that the Pronouncement carried you to this show barn. The herd you came from was not one born or bred of royalty or show breeding. In fact, if I remember correctly, they were quite rough and tumble. They were always looking for ways to resist what was being asked of them and rebelled at most of the human realm's contact."

"Yes, Your Highness, I am Lana," the bay mare confirmed. "I have been here now for three years and I am very grateful for that turn of events. It is true that my previous herd was a very rough crowd."

Still, Lana seemed tentative. Eponalisa softened as she read pain in the mare's hesitation.

"What is troubling you, dear one? Are you no longer happy with your Calling?"

"Oh, my yes," Lana cried. "I truly am. And I do not mean to be ungrateful. It is just that the other day I saw some of my old herd mates at an auction site by the show grounds. They called to me and I could tell they did not approve of how I was interacting with my human partners. I could feel that they thought I had changed and was no longer one of them." She continued sadly. "I tried to tell them how much I felt loved and cared for and how I liked being in this space, feeling proud of myself and what I was accomplishing."

"Go on," prompted Eponalisa.

The bay mare continued. "They did not believe me and seemed angry that I had changed, taunting me to come back to their herd. I have felt conflicted ever since I saw them."

Her head hung low in shame and confusion and she seemed to shrink in her stall. Eponalisa contemplated in silence before counseling the young mare. She wanted to remain sensitive to the mare's feelings, as the mare was struggling and felt lost.

"Lana, there is no turning back," she said as kindly as she could. "You see, you have grown, developed, and deepened on your life's journey. You now find yourself way down the trail from where you began. By making different choices and listening to your inner guidance, you have crafted a very different life for yourself.

"Your friends are asking you to undo all that you have become. It would make them feel better about themselves if you were to return to being who you once were. Who you were then was comfortable for them, for they did not need to grow or change to keep you or interact with you. Even today they continue to make poor choices over and over as if addicted to them."

Eponalisa picked up a brush from a box mounted just outside Lana's stall and began to brush Lana's shiny red coat. Her stroke was gentle and her intent was to provide comfort and assurance through the sense of touch.

Finally she added, "However, Lana, you have indeed grown and have moved onto new ground, soaring to new heights. For this, you should feel pride, not shame. Does this make sense to you Lana?"

"Yes, Your Highness," Lana replied, with more assurance in her voice.

"Lana, it's okay to look back. Looking back is reflective for you. Some yearning or nostalgia is to be expected. But trust that the new and higher ground upon which you stand is reward in itself. You are contributing to others in your life and making choices that support your happiness, health and joy."

The shiny mare loved feeling the brush upon her coat and listening to the fairy speaking to her.

"Keep moving forward, dear one. Just as in the human realm, when true growth occurs, there is no turning back," Eponalisa concluded.

"Thank you, Your Highness. It is so special to see you again. I choose to move forward and I will start right now. My rider is coming this morning for our lesson with the trainer and I will relish it with gratitude and joy!"

Eponalisa patted the young mare on the neck and gave her a soft kiss on her muzzle. After placing her dandy brush back in the box, she waved to her before leaving to meet up with Wisdom at his borrowed stall.

"Wisdom, are you done chomping that hay?" she teased. Wisdom kept grabbing large mouthfuls, knowing that they needed to scurry soon. Eponalisa unbraided his mane and tail and allowed them to flow free in giant curls of color. Although he was a dappled gray, his coat carried every color of the rainbow in its shine, almost like the prisms of a crystal. She tacked her dear friend for the day and finally pulled his head from the manger to place the bridle on his head. First, she had to pull gobs of hay from the sides of his mouth to make room for the bit. Then she slid the headstall over his ears. On the brow band hung a large, clear amethyst, which Eponalisa polished with a small rag before buckling the chinstrap.

She led her friend to the aisle and Wisdom bowed down upon a rubber grooming mat for her to mount him. Eponalisa adjusted her cloak and sat deep in her seat. She and Wisdom had met a barn full of new friends. She was grateful for this and for the black stallion's hospitality. She blew fairy dust on all the horses to bless them and waved her thanks to the black stallion as they prepared to leave.

Finally, they could hear the help coming. The farmhands talked easily back and forth about the big party they had attended the night before and the headaches they were each sporting as a result. Laughing as they opened the big end doors of the barn, they were completely unprepared for what they saw.

As soon as the space was large enough, Wisdom trotted forth through the opening. Carrying his mistress, he took off on a gallop to the edge of the farm. The men could not make out for sure exactly what they had seen. Eponalisa heard them exclaiming to each other in disbelief, laughing and teasing that they would take it easier in the parties to come. They shook their heads as the duo disappeared over the horizon. Eponalisa giggled as she heard one of them vow to never again drink beer!

CHAPTER THIRTEEN

Once out of sight, Eponalisa pulled Wisdom down to a soft jog. She felt relaxed and rested. She took great pleasure in the back and forth swaying of her hips to his rhythmic hoof beats. Wisdom could sense she was processing and simply needed his quiet companionship. They moved along together without a clear destination.

Refreshed from his bath and a good night's rest, Wisdom was warming up in the glow of the morning sunshine. His muscles felt strong and his mind was relaxed. He treasured these journeys each season with the fairy. Epona had certainly asked the correct young girl to complete the task this season.

Eponalisa felt hot tears of gratitude roll down her cheeks for the beauty around her. She had never taken the simple beauty of nature for granted. She loved the sweetness of the morning dew and the brilliant colors on the horizon as the sun showed off for another day. And she adored the hospitality of all the creatures who gathered along the pathway wherever they rode.

Gratitude. It was her sustenance and mantra this morning. For Eponalisa, there was nothing more powerful than experiencing gratitude, full and expressed gratitude for all the parts of her life. She looked again to the sky, then to the earth, and beheld the landscape before her. She was grateful for the beauty and wonder of the natural world. She was also thankful for the support she received through her good health and able body. She knew this was a true blessing and not one experienced by everyone. She never took her health for granted.

Thinking of her special partner, Wisdom, her heart swelled with love and gratitude for him. These journeys with him each season meant everything to her. She knew that all past journeys were but memories imparted by the Goddess Epona to the young woman chosen that season. And she knew that she had been given form through the young girl, Lisa. But the memories were now hers, as was the love and gratitude she felt.

She reflected on the willingness of the horse who had agreed to allow Epona to change him for the ride. Every season, Epona located the perfect duo to serve when they were embodied. That chosen duo would hold the magic, the past memories, the sacred knowledge, and the abilities for a short while to complete the mission. The horse, Clarity, had agreed to be transformed into the magical horse, Wisdom, for this brief time. She was grateful to Clarity for his trusting heart.

Eponalisa continued to take stock of all the things and beings she loved. Blessing each one silently, she trusted that each blessing would open up tenfold in the weeks of fall to come.

A couple of miles had gone by with both horse and rider lost in thought. Those thoughts were mingled with feelings and emotions about the journey and the preciousness of a new day. Eponalisa reached down to lovingly pat Wisdom on the neck. He felt soft and clean, just as he had in the beginning of their time together.

Spotting a tiny stream below them, she cued Wisdom to go down the embankment to the water's edge for a drink.

"There is some shade down there, my friend, and we can take a break before deciding where to ride to next."

Wisdom was surefooted as he found a place to make his descent. Eponalisa leaned back as far as she could to help him maintain his balance as he stepped down the steep embankment. Once at level ground, he walked to a space under the trees.

Bowing down for Eponalisa to dismount, Wisdom stretched out his right foreleg. When she was on the ground, Eponalisa removed his bridle. Then she took her silver chalice from its pouch to fill at the generous stream. After she had done so, Wisdom stepped down the bank, himself, and took his fill. Tasting the familiar sweetness of the water, he noted that they were only a few miles upstream from where they had begun their journey.

As he looked back to his mistress, he saw that she was again sitting on the soft ground. She had spread her deep purple cape on the grass, had drunk the water from her chalice, and was holding her scepter in her lap. Eyes closed and back erect, she sat very still, smiling sweetly, as if replaying a tender movie in her mind.

Happy, and always hungry, he went to graze a bit. He trusted that Eponalisa would find what she was looking for in her reverie

Eponalisa's vision was of the journey they had shared thus far. She thought of the beautiful herd of mares and foals they had first seen. She remembered the courageous alpha mare, Corrina, and her introduction to sweet Bridget. Bridget had paid the price and made the sacrifice to carry the Calling of Nurturance. Eponalisa knew she would carry it very well.

The fairy was deeply touched by the bravery and devotion she felt within the Belgian, Jeremiah. She knew he would carry the load for his human partner for as long as needed, allowing him to find the space to support his young daughter.

In her mind's eye, she could see the beautiful Snowbowl Meadow and the mighty leader, Dancer. She smiled as she thought of the Palomino mare, Sunny. Eponalisa was pleased that Sunny was already living out her Calling of Protection. She treasured having observed the mare as she carefully ushered her foal to the meadow, building her self-esteem while watching over her in the process. She admired how Sunny watched over the entire herd, from foals to elders, making sure they were all cared for. She could almost see angelic wings on her back.

A smile also found her lips when she remembered the antics and camaraderie of the logging mule team. She checked in with them internally and felt certain that they were having fun, regardless of the chores and tasks they were asked to perform.

The open hospitality of the black Friesian stallion was worthy of notice. How generous he had been!

She knew Albert would be having a day he would never forget as he was fully stepping into his Calling of Infinite Power. Eponalisa felt certain he would be famous one day and change many lives in the process.

Her heart felt calm and easy when she touched in with Lana. Lana was now moving forward again—no longer lost—and feeling grateful for the forward momentum in her life.

It had been quite a journey! Eponalisa felt that their work on this season's journey was almost complete. There was but one more visit to make as they began to make their way homeward.

Summoning Wisdom with a whistle, she laughed as he came, swiftly trotting over to her. She threw her arms around his neck and gave him a big hug. He drank in her sweetness and caressed her tightly with his neck. Tears formed and burned her eyes as she thought about how they would soon be parted.

Once back on the trail, Eponalisa ably cued Wisdom to follow a small deer trail that led up the steep side of the mountain. Leaning as far forward as she could to help him traverse the steep incline, she wrapped her fingers into his mane to avoid slipping off his back. The fairy intuitively knew that this was the trail to follow and felt a sudden sense of urgency.

As they climbed, Eponalisa saw the small herd of white-tailed deer watching them borrow their deer highway. The deer would cherish the blessing of her sparkling dust, which was covering the path as she passed. Wisdom wondered why these deer never created a straight line to follow and hoped they would be back on a wider trail soon.

"Thank you, Wisdom. I know that the deer trail is difficult. We might have taken an easier way. But I am feeling a sense of urgency to get to the flat meadow on top."

The trail leveled off and they finally reached the top. After resting a bit, so Wisdom could catch his breath, Eponalisa asked him to cross the rushing creek. Here, higher in the mountain, the creek was full and deep. The rocks were slick with moss and the icy water was swift, making it a challenge for even him to keep his balance. He lowered his head and took careful steps straight across.

The wet clay bank felt welcoming to him and he picked up a trot as soon as they left the water. Eponalisa seemed focused on finding a shortcut to her next Pronouncement.

As soon as the tiny herd of horses came into sight, Wisdom understood why his mistress was in a rush. He was glad to have been in service to her. A large sorrel mare was lying on the ground, surrounded by the tiny group.

Pacing back and forth was the elder grey gelding, Tobias. Wisdom recognized him from many of their rides over the years. Tobias was one of the oldest horses in the area. Yet, he was still as fit and capable as ever, despite a touch of arthritis now and again. Tobias perked his ears at their approach.

Eponalisa asked Wisdom to move next to a large rock a few yards south of the gathering so she could dismount and stand upon it. The tiny herd was so concerned about their friend on the ground, they failed to notice her arrival. Tobias, however, had, and was slowly making his way over to greet Wisdom and bow to the fairy. His head hung low and he seemed dejected.

"Our honor, Your Highness," he said as he bowed as far as his creaky knee would allow.

"Hello, Tobias. I came as quickly as I could to see you."

"Me? Why, I beg your pardon, Your Highness. But many years ago, I received my Pronouncement from the Goddess Epona," he politely reminded her. "I have tried to live it well."

Eponalisa smiled, mostly to herself, and then explained.

"Oh, I assure you that you have lived up to all expectations Tobias! Epona has always spoken well of you and how well you have honored your Calling."

After a few moments, she slowly continued.

"Now, as an elder, it is time for you to reinvent yourself. If you would like, Tobias, Epona has sent me to offer you another Calling."

Tobias became pensive. He thought of how the first Pronouncement had given him so much clarity about the path he was to follow in his life. He reflected on how many times he had made choices over the course of his life. He had used the pronouncement as a beacon to clarify what was expected of him and light the way to its fulfillment.

Finally, he told Eponalisa that he would be open to reinvention if that was meant to be for him.

Eponalisa smiled and said, "Your Reinvented Calling is one that cannot be given to the young. It can only be bestowed on those who have been on the Earth for a long time. And it is only given to those who have been open to learning their lessons along the way. Would you be open to receiving it, Tobias?"

Humbly, Tobias returned, "Why, yes, I am again honored to be seen as worthy."

With that, Eponalisa set to work. First, she drew from her purple velvet pouch a bundle of dried sage tied with palomino horsehair. She also withdrew her tiny box of wooden matches. Carefully striking a match, she lit the dried bundle, blowing on it to create a low flame. She allowed it to burn for a full minute and then blew the flame out to create a smoke stream that continued to emit from it. Pulling a pink and green abalone shell from her bag, she was prepared to work. The beautiful shell would catch the sage ashes.

Eponalisa began to work around Tobias. Fluttering her wings, she slowly flew around his entire body, bathing Tobias with the pungent sage smoke. She moved the smoke around the older horse's neck and back. She carefully covered each leg before moving on to his chest and spine and gave special attention to his heart area. The entire process took several minutes. Throughout it, she asked that he be allowed to release all the emotional pain from everything he had seen in his lifetime, while retaining the wisdom and life lessons. Further, she asked that he be able to pass on his greatest knowledge and comfort to others, ministering to them.

Tobias was still, silent, and trusting as she worked all around him. He smelled the strong scent of the sage, which sparked a memory from his time as a colt. One of his herd's elders had smelled the same way when his father had passed over. The bittersweet memory had lingered to this day. He felt his heart lighten as she spoke.

"Tobias, the herd is concerned about the mare who is dying. Correct?"

"Yes, Eponalisa. She has a terrible bellyache. It is persistent and I am more aware than the others of what it will mean for her in the next few hours," he said, shedding a tear for her.

"Tobias, you are about to receive and carry the Calling of Sage Wisdom. Completing a cycle in your long life, you are experiencing an ending of your own youth and adulthood at this time. Your vast accumulated wisdom and understanding are being called upon now. You are a sage member of the herd," Eponalisa explained. "You are encouraged to remember and use all of the lessons you have learned thus far on your own life's journey," she continued.

"You will meet many in the human realm who are grieving losses of their own. They will be healed through your loving energy and find their way to lessons they must also learn."

Slowly, and with great patience, she furthered his acceptance and understanding of what was being asked of him.

"The herd is surely experiencing tragedy today and will feel much grief and bitter disappointment. As an elder, you know that this is simply a part of life. And your own long life has taught you that grief provides contrast for the joy that will surely follow. Great lessons are learned at these times, Tobias. The lessons are often hidden behind the drama and overt energies present in the situation."

Softly, she counseled, "As you assume responsibility for being the sage of the herd, it is your job to counsel them. Through your life experience, you know that sadness is provided as contrast. You know, too, that it is always matched in the future by an equal measure and intensity of success and joy."

Tobias nodded in understanding, then said to her, "Endings can be painful and grief a strong presence.

I have learned the importance of expressing my emotions and not suppressing or hiding my pain."

Eponalisa was grateful that he fully understood.

"Go now to comfort the herd, Tobias. I am so sorry that the young mare is passing over and so grateful that you are present for all of them. This great learning will help them all to make it through their grief."

Eponalisa then returned to Wisdom, whose head hung low. For once, he was not interested in grazing. She mounted gently. They stood quietly and observed as Tobias moved silently back to the herd.

As he reentered their circle around the sorrel mare, it was clear that she was taking her last few breaths. A young colt asked, "Oh, whatever can we do, Tobias?"

"Son," he said quietly, "allow your pain to flow freely from your being. As a herd, we must do so. With this expression of our pain, we honor the full experience of this beautiful friend's life. In time, we will heal. We will treasure her memory forever. And we will be ready to let go when the time is right. That time is not now. Now is the time to let in our own pain and endure it together."

The tiny herd pulled closer in their circle and Eponalisa could hear him saying to them, "Call upon all that comforts you at this time. Call upon your faith and trust what is. Trust that this ending is only a new beginning for our friend. And this time will create an opening for lush new beginnings in the days to come. We have been blessed to know this mare, our friend. From her love, one day new blessings will pour forth in her honor."

Eponalisa and Wisdom departed as quietly as they came, leaving the tiny herd to suffer their loss and hold their memorial in privacy. The magical duo took with them the knowledge that Tobias would shepherd the herd through the painful lesson.

CHAPTER FOURTEEN

Tracing back over the trail and trekking back across the deep creek, the pair rode in reverent silence. Eponalisa had already told Wisdom they were in no hurry now and could take the old jeep trail back in lieu of the deer trail.

Relieved, Wisdom felt waves of déjà vu stirring within him. He knew they were close to the end of their present journey, as he was experiencing familiar feelings that he recognized from previous times with the fairy.

He would soon see his mate, Grace. He caught the scent in his large nostrils, long before either he or Eponalisa saw her. He knew she was close by. He could feel his heart quicken. Although as a stallion, Wisdom had sired many foals, he trusted that he had found his lifetime soul mate in Grace. Her scent was unlike any other mare for him and often caused his mighty heart to not just quicken, but skip a complete beat.

The fence line began alongside the jeep trail. The farm's north fence line ran for several miles and it looked as if the horses were turned out to graze in the outer pasture today. The huge pasture had been off-limits during the autumn months to allow foliage protection. As Wisdom jogged along the fence line, he heard her call to him—a long melodious neigh of familiarity.

Eponalisa smiled ear to ear. She could feel Wisdom's excitement in seeing his mate. The fairy was also anxious because she was about to surprise her old friend with a special Pronouncement for his chosen one.

Grace was sleek and fine, with a coat the color of maple syrup. Large liquid dark brown eyes, a small dish shape to her face, and beautiful bone structure were clearly her assets. Her long mane and tail were a glossy, shiny black and seemed almost fluid as she moved. She was far more than just a bay in Wisdom's eyes.

Wisdom called out to Grace in alto tones. Eponalisa could feel his chest swell and his neck puff up. An extra beat was suddenly in his jog. The fine mare ran to meet them at the fence line and fell in step, with only the fence between them. Neither saw anything but the other.

Eponalisa was thrilled for her dear friend and could feel his pleasure at seeing his mate.

"I suppose we could take a break, if you want to take a moment to say hello," Eponalisa said in formality, wondering to herself if there was really any choice about the matter.

This was happy news to both Wisdom and the bay mare, Grace, as they both turned to walk right up to the fence line. The mare quickly put her head over the fence, with the top rail at her jaw line. Wisdom called again to her and met her nuzzle enthusiastically. A moment later, nose to nose, he was able to share with her how glad he was to see her feeling well and enjoying the fall day.

After a few moments of visiting, Wisdom regained his composure and took a large step back.

"Your Highness, may I present Grace to you?" he asked.

Eponalisa smiled in response and said, "I would be honored."

"Grace, this is the Fairy Eponalisa," Wisdom said, trying to remember his best manners.

Grace had already known who was aboard him and was embarrassed by her own behavior. Her joy in seeing Wisdom had overtaken her and she had forgotten her manners. Immediately, she bowed down with the elegance and coordination of a ballet dancer. She did this in full respect, hoping that Eponalisa would forgive her for having forgotten everything with the mere sight of her beau, Wisdom.

"Grace," Eponalisa said, smiling. "Grace," the name flowed from her tongue as she repeated it.

"Why, how wise your partners in the human realm were at your birth! The name suits you."

Eponalisa squeezed her mount's sides with her calves.

"Wisdom, allow me to come closer to the fence line, please. I have a Pronouncement to deliver to Grace from Epona."

Almost stumbling, Wisdom's heart swelled suddenly in his huge chest. He felt as if it would burst! He had never felt such pride or joy. He knew how very special his mare, Grace, was and that she was worthy of this ritual. But his partner had truly caught him off guard.

Eponalisa stayed seated upon his back and leaned over the fence rail to appraise the fineness of her friend's chosen one. "Yes, indeed, Grace, your very Calling from the Goddess Epona herself is that of Grace. You have received Grace and many natural gifts have been bestowed upon you. Now is the time when you are called to heighten your awareness of all the ways Grace shows itself in your life. Note that some are small distinctions, while others show up as talents beyond measure."

The fairy stopped for a moment as Grace listened in rapt attention. Then she joyfully continued.

"Your Grace is uniquely your own. Some aspects of your personal Grace remain unknown to you at this time. Now is the moment to explore and discover the depths within you."

The mare was both attentive and fascinated with what Eponalisa was sharing. She swelled inside, feeling validated by what was being said.

"Today is the perfect time to honor all with which you are naturally blessed and stand in gratitude for it," Eponalisa added.

The mare stood still and silent. She had been deeply moved by the Pronouncement. She had been given the name Grace when she was a week old. Her mother had been killed in a tragic barn fire, yet through Grace, she had somehow escaped and survived. She had been named for this miracle.

When the mare had gathered her composure again, Eponalisa continued tenderly.

"Grace, you are now asked to help others, both in your realm and the human realm, to discover their own hidden talents and truly recognize them as their Grace. Do you understand?"

"Yes, Your Highness. I have been truly blessed and have tried to never take it for granted. We all have so much to share. I will continue to do all that I can to shine a light on each individual's special natural gifts, so that they may recognize them and give thanks."

Eponalisa bent forward on Wisdom's neck and retrieved a small cobalt blue glass vial from a leather pouch hanging from his jeweled collar. Wisdom was standing stone still, even though he was bursting with desire to move. The sweet fairy uncorked the vial and brought it to her tiny nose. She took a deep breath of the essential oil. It was made of several flower essences and had been imbued by Epona with the very scent of the Angels.

Asking Wisdom to side pass to the fence, she now sat before the mare's lovely face. Tipping the vial, her tiny fingers received drops of the oil before touching them to Grace's broad forehead. The mare's small white star absorbed the oils, causing a sweet spiral to form in the hair pattern. After the ritual was complete, the trio looked to the sky and stood in silence for several minutes, in gratitude to their maker.

Grace was immensely moved. Her liquid eyes showed Eponalisa that she felt a deep understanding of what the silence held.

Satisfied, Eponalisa asked Wisdom to continue down the fence line. He did not hesitate, for he understood the importance of their work. Grace accompanied the pair until the fence line ended. Wisdom assured her he would see her soon and with that, the pair continued on.

Wisdom had always known his mate was special. Yet, to have it recognized by Epona and honored by

Eponalisa touched his soul deeply. As they rode on, Wisdom silently sent waves of gratitude and love to Eponalisa.

Part III:
The Return

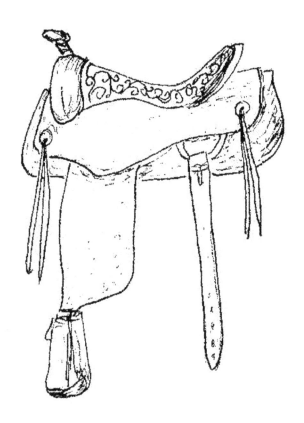

CHAPTER FIFTEEN

Eponalisa felt complete and ready to return to Epona. Another half mile and they would be back to the rock where the fall journey had begun. The time together had passed quickly and the day's sun had begun to set, turning the horizon shades of orange and pink. It reminded Eponalisa of the colors of sherbet. She enjoyed the show and allowed her mount to daydream.

As they approached the mounting rock, Wisdom's ears perked fully forward in recognition of the silver cloud floating across the ground toward them. He knew this would be the goddess, herself. He felt conflicted. He was ready to meet her again. At the same time, he was not yet ready to say farewell to his fairy partner.

Sidling up to the rock, he could feel the fairy echoing his emotions. It would be a long while before they rode together again. Eponalisa patted his neck and slid daintily onto the table rock.

As she began to curtsy and Wisdom bent low in a magnificent bow, the goddess appeared before them. The beautiful smile on her face seemed to ripple throughout her shimmering body. Her divine mission having been fully and beautifully completed, she appeared content.

"Please rise, sweet ones, for I am so pleased with all you have accomplished in this short time. Together, you have fulfilled my work beyond measure. You rode together as a caring force, guiding all those you met. You created a force for love and the fulfillment of destiny that will benefit humankind from this day forth."

Her voice sounded like the tinkle of perfect musical notes and it took but a glimpse of her to know that this was the presence of pure white light and love.

"Are you ready to part for now so that I may bring back the sweet child and her trusty mount?"

Eponalisa again hugged her mighty Wisdom. "I will see you again soon and dream of you every night until then."

Wisdom felt his cheeks fill with heat as he nuzzled her gently.

With that, the goddess blew a deep purple cloud of dust to cover them both. As the dust began to clear, Lisa felt her mind clear as well. Like awakening from a long afternoon nap, still drowsy yet fully rested, she began to look around her.

Lisa's surroundings were familiar but her sense of herself was not. Holding tightly to Clarity's bridle reins and feeling the table rock beneath her feet, she could not believe all that had happened. Had she dreamed it? Was she daydreaming? She thought not, as she was inexplicably in the presence of a goddess!

"Dear ones, welcome back," the goddess said in her most melodious manner. "Thank you, on behalf of all the horses in the Equine Realm. The two of you have done a fine job. You were courageous and true to the task put before you."

The Goddess Epona paused, giving Lisa a chance to gather her wits . . . and her memories. "Do you remember your time spent in this form?" the Goddess asked.

Lisa cleared her throat, as if she had not spoken in days.

"Why, yes, I think so. It feels like a dream, but more clear and present. I feel different, or changed somehow."

Clarity sneezed and nodded his head in agreement.

"You are different and forever changed, my dear. You now hold the understanding of many of life's truths. You have learned the importance of Nurturance and Protection. You have witnessed the blessing of Grace. You have felt the freedom to move forward and never turn back. And you have taken joy in the camaraderie that you share every day with Clarity.

"You both have grown and will be rewarded in many ways for your service. This magical private journey will not be one you will be able to explain convincingly to others. There will be no words for it, nor ears capable of hearing them. You see, it was for the two of you alone. But always know and trust that the journey was, in fact, real and that you performed a wondrous service for many horses in the process.

"You must run along now. Your family will be looking for you. Move always in love and light."

As she spoke these words, the goddess began to move back into the silver cloud. Before Lisa could say a word in response, Epona floated away along the ground, disappearing over the horizon.

Lisa grabbed at the horn of her saddle and climbed aboard Clarity. She felt the firmness of suede saddle seat and the warmth of Clarity's body bringing her back into reality, more and more each moment.

She paused, wondering if this was reality. Was her familiar form as Lisa reality? Was it the only reality? Or had the goddess been right? Had her embodiment as Eponalisa been real, too? Had her journey been real? Was Clarity the horse she knew so well, or was he also Wisdom?

She rode to the gate and found that it opened as if by magic for them to cross through, back onto the farm property. Lisa heard a soft, gentle laugh as they did so. She spun around, expecting to find that the goddess had returned. She wanted to ask her to be sure to lock it as Paul always requested. But no one was there. Lisa looked all around, but the beautiful goddess was nowhere to be found.

Clarity's tummy growl was the next audible sound. Lisa laughed out loud. He was always hungry! She saw that he was looking far off in the distance to his own barn. It appeared to be feeding time!

"Okay, let's go, Clarity."

And with that, the two began to move at a trot along the pathway to their barn. Everything looked the same and, yet, somehow different. Lisa could not quite explain it to herself.

Lisa bathed Clarity, put liniment on his legs, and wrapped them in support bandages. The bandages would soothe his muscles and keep him sound. She giggled as he rolled in the fresh sawdust. She had a vague sense of déjà vu as she watched him rolling in the stall. Next, Lisa put away all of her tack, cleaning it with a cloth as she went. Once his saddle was on its stand and his bridle was on its hook in the tack room, she returned to Clarity's stall.

Opening the door, she stepped inside to hug him as hard as she could and thank him for the day's adventure.

"Clarity, you may not be a magical mighty steed

like the stallion Wisdom, but every cell of your being is full of love and loyalty. I would not want you any other way."

Lisa heard Nana's car in the farm driveway and could not wait to tell her all about their day. Clarity took a big bite of his hay and then went to speak through the stall wall to his best friend next door. She was a lovely bay mare and he thought she was the most graceful mare he had ever seen.

CHAPTER SIXTEEN

Lisa was so excited when Nana picked her up at the farm, she could hardly contain herself.

"Hold on, young lady," Nana pleaded as she laughed. "Let's get home and get you to the shower. Then you can share all about it over dinner, okay? I thought you might be famished from your day's adventure. I made spaghetti for dinner."

Lisa thought it sounded like a perfect plan.

In her nightgown and with her tummy full, she stayed up most of the night telling Nana every detail she could remember. When she started to doze off, Nana tucked a quilt over her on the sofa, kissed her cheek, and told her she should write it all down in her journal. It was a terrific story.

Lisa's parents returned from their trip the following evening. Lisa hugged Nana good-bye and, wishing she could ditch school and spend the day with Clarity instead, she prepared to finish her homework for the next day.

When her parents asked her how her weekend had been, Lisa simply said, "It was so fantastic, you would never believe me!" Then she hugged them both and went to her room to write in her journal.

Dear Me,

    I am home again, about to snug into my soft bed, under clean sheets. I missed my room. I plan to explore my dreams in a new way!

    I know that this time spent as Eponalisa was not a dream but a real life adventure. An adventure neither Clarity nor I will ever forget. I know now that my future will always hold being with horses and although I am not yet sure in what way, I will follow my own Calling. I now see that my parents will one day understand what is true for me. Divine time will give me the answers I seek and Divine time will give my parents the understanding I want from them.

    With this gift of knowledge, I find my own happiness in all that I choose to do. I can't say exactly how, but I feel so different, calm and clear. I trust that my dreams are actually much more than dreams. They are my vision of what

I could create and the future
I am invited to enter.
   Yawning now . . . I am ready to
sleep and start fresh tomorrow,
stepping into my future.
Lisa

ABOUT THE AUTHOR

Inspired by her relation-ship with horses and her profession in psychother-apy, Melisa Pearce founded her company, Touched by a Horse™, in 1998. For more than thirty years, Melisa has bred, raised, and shown horses. She maintains ranches in both Arizona and Colorado.

Melisa's BSW and MSW degrees from Arizona State University led her to a career in private practice that has included a training institute, developed with partners, for a 400-hour certification in Experiential Therapy. In 1982, Melisa began creating her unique therapeutic approach to human emotional healing through interactive work with both a therapist and a therapy horse. Melisa's passion is teaching others how to facilitate emotional healing and exploration of self through the interaction of horses.

Melisa is proud to be a clinician at the Equine Affaire and the Equine Extravaganza. In 2008, she was selected as one of the Top 50 Influential Horsewomen in the US. Her spiritual retreats were selected for the top honor of Best Spiritual Retreat by *5280 Magazine* (Denver) in 2007. Her website includes articles on her work from *Paint Horse Journal, Northwest Woman Magazine, Body + Soul magazine, American Cowboy magazine, Eagle Valley News,* and *Healing Path Magazine.*

As an author, she has written for several magazines, has created the inspirational card deck, *Whispers from a Horse's Heart* and has recorded her own Wisdom's Journey CDs: *Wisdom's Journey to your Personal Future, Wisdom's Journey to the Chaka's* and *Wisdom's Journey to Abundance.* She also co-authored the book, *Games People Play with Horses,* a guide to sixty interactive exercises for equine work.

Eponalisa is Melisa's first novel.

Melisa Pearce lives near Niwot, Colorado on Lil Bit North Ranch with her sweetheart, Dane, one miniature horse (Pepper), one miniature donkey (Bitsy), two alpacas (Brownie and Blackie), a paint stallion, eight assorted horses, two Bernese Mountain Dogs (Odot and Harley), one Pembroke Welsh Corgie (Dinky), one barn cat, a blue heron, and two ducks.

AN INVITATION

Dear Reader,

You are cordially invited to visit us on our website, http://www.touchedbyahorse.com.

If you loved Wisdom in *Eponalisa*, be sure to sign up online for his free inspirational email messages (one, three, or five times a week). You can also choose one of two posters to print, free of charge, and subscribe to our quarterly newsletter.

If you want even more of Wisdom and his friends, you can also find it online on my *Whispers from a Horse's Heart* inspiration cards and the *Wisdom's Journey* CDs.

Our online store is also chock-full of fun equine gifts for you and your friends. I personally search gift shows around the country for just the right quality and assortment of items, from jewelry and other accessories to beautiful Trail of Painted Ponies figures.

I would also like to invite you to contact me through our website or email me directly at Melisa@TouchedByAHorse.com to inquire about attending our retreats or workshops, to book a private session, or to invite me to speak at your conference or meeting. If you would like to see our facilities, you can take a virtual tour online. Just click on "Ranch Tour."

In Synergy,
Melisa